2031

A New World

Collision

Episode One

jack torn

ISBN: 978-0-6458863-9-9

Global Daze

To Cruiser - Gene

Contents

Part One

Pinn

1.

Pinn was sitting on a bench overlooking Maleogle beach from an elevated park on the northern side when he was joined by a fellow dressed as a lumberjack who, he learnt later, was OyOyann. His name was Bruce. Pinn pretended he was still alone.

Shortly Bruce spoke.

"It's your turn, lost soul, to smooch the Z∞∞a."

"What makes you think I have lost anything, big guy," said Pinn without turning his head? "I am a unit of arguable consciousness answerable only to the connections I make."

"Cute," said Bruce. "You need a grease and oil change."

"No thank you, pervert."

It was a fine spring morning, no longer brisk. Neither moved much on the bench. Both looked beachward, legs outstretched, hands pocketed in jeans.

"So, let's begin," began Bruce. "I grant thee three wishes."

"Thee does not want them," said Pinn.

"Not so much wishes as do overs."

"I don't want them."

"You may choose three occasions from your apparent past where you would have acted differently, revisit the events one by one and do as you wished you had done, or dreamed you did do, whatever. The portal into the past lasts exactly nine hours, after which time you will be flung back to now, noon, October 11, 2024, bringing with you the changes your decisions make to your environment and status, and the aches and pains of being manhandled by time. Upon your return from the first re-experience, you must choose the starting point for the next re-experience within one hundred and eighty minutes, the third within ninety minutes. Not much time really. Failure to do so will result in nonexistence.

"It should be pointed out also," continued Bruce, "changing your decisions, as you have and will, may wipe some or all of the memories of the life you know now and replace them with entirely different ones. It can be a good thing but it's tricky. I am not here to help. I am here to facilitate."

"Even unwantedly?"

"Indeed, you have been chosen."

"By whom?"

"Not by whom, why?"

"Ok, why, but still, by whom?"

"Genetics. Back in the day when the second and third chromosome were fused to adjust consciousness to breed a slightly brighter race so the higher would not have to be so involved in the day to day running of the place, they went slightly beyond. Long story short, all that time ago, your great, great grandfather, quite a few thousand years removed, during those experiments, was one of only one who was given the amino acid, *Zeta*-E- methylamino -*A*-alanine-L (ZEAL). It's in your gene pool along with about a million others but is not switched on and will not be until a certain chaos is reached. Our analysts, however, recently discovered that by then it will be too late, hence the intervention."

"Really? In my lifetime?"

"Yesss...Maybe."

"Bullshit."

"Gesundheit," said Bruce. "It's out of your hands Pinn. An upgrade is required. The original coding for this planet's current race, as it turns out, was unjustifiably celebrated. It shouldn't have been. We have since fed the coders to the lions but now, at the twenty-third hour, we are hoping to make a manual adjustment because your planet is about to go through a trying journey and for some of the race to survive, we need some heavy-duty knuckle draggers who can still scratch where it itches."

"Flattery now."

"Think of this process you are about to undergo as an upgrade and reboot. It can be quite painless. In your regressions you will find the right path, or we will attempt to find it for you. Think procreation. That is all I can say."

Pinn continued to protest. Bruce vanished. Pinn found himself seated at a window in an empty black and gold restaurant at tree top level. He was attended by a Walking Dead version of Quasimodo who grunted and handed him a glossy white sheet with 5D monochromatic lettering that read; choose your first stop, boldly at the top, you have sixty-three seconds to do so starting now, in much smaller print below. Both were centered, no caps.

The disclaimer at the bottom, also centered, no caps, no longer bold and in a smaller font still, pointed out the incumbent's illusion of choice would only continue in the air of cooperation.

Wish Won

Pinn and George got together because Pinn's sister knew Sugar, George's wife. Sugar and George had just moved from Canada to Cronulla. George got transferred to the antipodes by the energy company that employed him as some sort of punishment. Sugar was saying to Pinn's sister, both swimming instructors, they had no friends, and during one conversation mentioned George played guitar. Pinn, at the time, was enthusiastic about playing guitar too. The two girls decided to introduce the two boys.

The day came. Pinn's sister was not present. Something came up for her so Pinn and his instrument turned up alone. Brave for the awkward teen. After a cup of tea, the boys showed each other theirs, tinkered about tuning, found hierarchy, and moved on.

In the following months the relationship grew. Pinn began to visit George and Sugar's apartment two or three times a week. George and Pinn would play guitar, drink, and make merry. Sugar would only get annoyed if she could not get the children to settle.

Sugar was a diminutive, shapely woman with long, blond hair and clear eyes. She had a stirring influence on the boy. She was a reason he agreed to meet George when his sister suggested it. He had seen her at the pool in her bathers.

George was short like his wife, had a big smile under a Mexican mustache and a wicked laugh. But he was a man in turmoil. Soon after Pinn made his acquaintance George began a surprising number of affairs about which he liked to boast. Naive Pinn listened to his stories of conquest in awe hoping to find vindication for the lustful thoughts he had been having about his wife.

Everything blew up in the end. Sugar found out about Georges philandering one afternoon when she came home to find her husband's cock, to use avian analogy, playing amongst the babysitter's tits. The kids were at school. The babysitter was visiting from the apartment upstairs. George was on a day off which is why Sugar wangled an early finish. At first, it looked like they would work it out, but a week later they were separated. A week after that, without saying a word to anyone, George and the children got on a plane to Edmonton.

Friday night, one week prior to his departure and one week after exposure, all three attended a family birthday party for Delores, Pinn's sister, at Pinn's mother's house.

Everyone except George was looking forward to it.

George's reasons for not looking forward to it were Mrs. Prïck, Shirley, hated him, and that the B sisters – Pinky and Blossom were likely to be present. The latter did cause George some consternation later in the evening as things wound up, but it was the lesser of the revelations for him that night.

It was on this night, all those years ago, Pinn wanted to, but did not have the courage to embrace his dark side. Courtesy of the OyOyann, he was getting another chance.

*

Sugar wanted to dance, drink and be young again. She wanted to forget and have fun. She flirted with the boy who she had taught over previous months to wash more frequently, and others.

Pinn remembers drinking too much and feeling guilty. His mother's friend, a tall, dark, dick with a harelip named Dirk from the local constabulary turned up just when joints were being passed around. It took no sleuth to know it. She hadn't invited him but knew he would attend and said so. She was not happy. She thought her children's behavior imprudent. A dick is always a dick she said.

Somehow, Pinn and Sugar found themselves alone in a room used as an office.

Pinn escaped to the room. He was drunk, stoned, and feeling uncomfortable with Sugar's attention and George's low growl whenever he went near. He half sat on the desk and lit a cigarette. There was a lamp on in the corner behind a low-legged, modestly cushioned, high-backed, red, couch. He was just pocketing his lighter when Sugar entered.

It was a knowing turning of the knob upon entry and a certain click, at breach, as she arsed the door shut. No, she arched her back, her hands behind her on the knob, and then lent to click.

Here, the first time, young Pinn unceremoniously fled.

On OyOyann time, he didn't. He timed out.

There were twenty minutes left on the 'do over' clock when Pinn found himself alone with Sugar. Alone with Sugar was something Pinn's fantasies had embraced since he first saw her golden smile as she leant forward to scoop up a dogpaddling child.

Pinn tried not to ogle. He knew what she was wearing, he was at their flat when she dressed. Large, thin, silver, hoop earrings, a cheesecloth top, a white studded belt, tight, tight jeans and red cowgirl boots with little mirrors on them. Her hair was down at first but while standing at the door she materialized a tie from somewhere and deliberately fashioned a ponytail. The opaque material, the process, the lighting, truly enchanted young Pinn who dripped to his knees.

Sugar stepped closer, knelt, and leaned forward as if to scoop up a dog-paddling child but withdrew when Pinn fidgeted adversely. She smelt like pink marshmallows, her eyes invited, and her lips were painted the same red as her boots.

"The crime has already been committed," confessed Pinn fumbling for a cigarette though he hadn't finished his last.

"What crime," asked Sugar?

"George knows this is going on," said Pinn, "I love you and I have abused you shamelessly over and over in my mind since the time I first saw you. I betray, have betrayed George every time."

He dropped his eyes.

"Who cares about George," said Sugar putting her right, crooked, index with a pink painted nail under his chin to raise his head. "For your information, mummy's boy, little man, you only love parts of me. You have wanted to conquer. Conquer. I want to be conquered."

Pinn didn't.

To his possible credit, with Sugar's insistence, he was getting pretty wound up when George burst through the door three seconds before the closure of the portal to see his wife and Pinn crash onto the couch, which then toppled over. By the time George got across the room both were gone.

2.

"You wanted to play," said Bruce. "Why not? Probably best you didn't get to the ice cave."

"I have no idea what you are talking about," said Pinn. "It's drizzling unlike before and I am walking a huge dog. I didn't know I had a dog. I am no longer married to Nerinda but to Meridiana who, in my previous life was my stepsister. I now have only two children as opposed to three. What happened to the other one?"

"You will be completely orientated in your new role in a few more minutes Pinn. Be patient," said the OyOyann. "It may be quicker next time. You will remember nothing of the old. Me, only vaguely. But we will meet again soon."

*

OyOyann began turning up on social media in 2024. Considered gods, they were recognizable by their height, narrowed eyes, and forked tongues. They tended to scratch their palms too. They were elusive in that their ecologically sustainable, Earth existence depended on, for whatever reason, a human population dilution limit of about one in a billion. There were eight, possibly nine, OyOyann worldwide by the time they were noticed.

Some consider the above more of a conspiracy theory. There were not nine OyOyann all dressed as lumberjacks calling themselves Bruce, hawking the same product with the same forked tongue and itchy palm. There was one.

According to Dr. Seknd Okazaki, a self-proclaimed expert on the subject, omitting the Nephilim and a pretty neat, evidential timeline, the OyOyann, once again, wish to modify the human chromosome suite. They need the same thing they did the last time they were here. They foresee an ebb in the life cycle for the planet on the horizon and are hoping to facilitate a few survivors.

Posting homo sapiens through multidimensional space to achieve "go, stop, return," time manipulation and allow the subject to switch to another thread exposes the organism to bugs and diseases that do not exist in their normal plane. Despite that, in the brief time the OyOyann force the trespass, chances of anyone catching anything are minimal, says Dr. Okazaki. However, she argues, "They do want the subject to genetically progress."

It gets complicated from there. It has something to do with a ridiculous chance of simultaneous astengols occurring in a flixenal region the instant before time now, squared, conspires with consciousness, in the subject's ajna.

For the fantastically minded, if the site hasn't been taken down, more details about the OyOyann can be found at http://www.sekndokazaki/glifstremnt48a/just/so!

The OyOyann story, as documented on various blogs, went like this: The OyOyann, a tall fellow dressed like a lumberjack, who calls himself Bruce (Baal Zevuv according to one blogger), turns up in some unsuspecting person's life and offers three do-overs.

"No one comes back," according to David Gale.

*

Pinn was fighting with Meridiana, which is why he was out walking the dog. He didn't know why he was fighting with her yet, but he did remember, earlier in the day, he had promised Nerinda croissants. He didn't have croissants, but he was close to his old address and decided to visit. It was a left turn one block back from the beach, then up the hill a bit on the other side. The house had a better view of the park than the shoreline.

It took him fifteen minutes at a distracted pace. He allowed the lunging and nosey animal only one pee stop, though he took countless others before Pinn reached the home he owned less than an hour earlier. He did not hesitate. He bounded up the twelve steps from the street to the terrace in threes, surprising the dog, then walked toward the sliding glass door expecting it to recognize him and open. It didn't and didn't.

Looking down at impact, Pinn's experience was of orbiting Saturnian moons in an unseeing disorientated feelinglessness. He staggered a few steps backward and dropped the dog leash. He felt he should sit.

He found his way safely back to the steps, sat on the top one, lent back, and passed out. There was a little bit of an ocean view to the right.

After what seemed an instant, he woke with a start when the OyOyann kicked his boot and said in a drill sergeant drawl, "This ain't no time to be lying down sonny."

Pinn's startled wake involved an overly ineffective reflex and a shriek. He gathered himself, crossly, quickly. "How much time do I have," Pinn heard himself ask?

"Twenty-seven minutes," said Bruce. "Let's get to the bench."

"What's the hurry?" Pinn queried. "The bench is only fifteen minutes away."

"Let's go," Bruce repeated starting down the steps.

The dog is forgotten here. Just as Pinn lay down and his head went back his peripheral vision picked up the door opening and the dog trotting in.

Bruce waited on the curb for Pinn who was in no hurry. Eventually, they met up. When there was a break in the moderate late morning traffic, they crossed the road. The drizzle, which had stopped, resumed.

Bruce strode as if on a mission and Pinn had to jog every other step to keep up. It was not so bad between intersections because they had to slow down to wait for lights to change, but once they crossed the road and entered the expansive, upward-sloping parkland, Pinn gave up trying to keep up and stopped to smoke a cigarette and catch his breath. He sat on the grass under a tree thirty feet from a bus stop.

After a while, Pinn continued on his way. He felt all right. He knew Meridiana would not be upset when he got back if he spent a little time out of the house. She would cool. It was a simple space hook gaff. He thought he might sit a few minutes, then return home.

Pinn was deep in thought, so he didn't see the big fellow sitting on the normally empty bench until he'd already committed himself to sit on it.

Shortly, Bruce spoke.

"We are not looking for wimps Pinn. We would feel more confident about you had you fulfilled your want. Not to worry. There is still hope. Two left; where to now?"

"Your name is Bruce, right?" said Pinn looking at a silly gull held up by the breeze, whose interest was caught by a rolling wrapper. "I have no idea."

"You know nothing about your current life?"

"I know I am married to Meridiana who is cranky with me. We have two children and a dog. I know I crashed into a door and took a timeless, dreamless nap for about sixty minutes that felt like a second to me."

"Trying to visit a wife you never had."

"Whatever. Why does my backside feel like it has been corked and there is a thick feeling in my neck?"

"The neck thing is because you recently head-butted a sturdy glass door. The other has to do with the slingshot nature of pro-particle transfer. It was mentioned earlier. You have no place you want to revisit?"

"None."

Bruce stood leisurely. He wore a kind of petaled watch on his inside right wrist. When Pinn first noticed it, before the first regression, he thought it decorative. The figuring was turquoise with silver highlights on black. It was now all a luminous amber.

"It's been nice knowing you Pinn," said Bruce, grinning almost goofishly. "My device changing to amber indicates you are in your last forty-eight hundred seconds of life. And you know what that means."

"Harsh Bruce," said Pinn. "Maybe I lost my memory when I hit my head. Not my fault."

Bruce grinned again, took his hands out of his front pockets, put them in his back pockets, dropped his head and scuffed a tuft of grass growing through a crack in the cement.

"Arguable to me Pinn," said Bruce, "but since you said it, it is good enough for our law. Maybe you did lose that memory. Maybe you didn't. The growing "#not you too," movement is beginning to gain attention in some unwanted places. I am trying to mitigate that perception."

Slowly, he resumed his seat. His hands went to his knees. The petals at his wrist changed to carmine. Three hundred and sixty seconds left.

"What I can offer you Pinn, for your second revisit, and it can only be offered here, now, is that I choose the next moment for you. For varying reasons, I cannot choose the third. To continue, say yes, or no."

"Do I get context before I go?"

"No. It's further back than the last time. It will come to you once you get there. You will have to choose for yourself after this return, and in shorter time. Yes, or no?"

"Tell me again how you get to do this to me."

"It's my job. I can quote a job number if you would like."

"Really?"

Bruce's petals turned chocolate cosmos with gold highlights and the background turned scarlet. Two hundred and forty seconds.

"Yes, or no?"

"So, you are saying, in essence, we are slaves."

"I can't say I made that leap Pinn, but we are all slaves if that's the way you want to go. We are in a whole, and in a unit of the whole, all at the same time, over and over again, and each unit has its own hierarchy. Ignoring good, evil, countless other motivators and illnesses, any personal slavishness you may feel depends largely upon the level you think you are indebted to your unit for the energy you have consumed and not replaced. Or something like that. But who cares?

"Very soon the redness of my device will turn imperial, indicating you have less than one hundred and twenty seconds to live. I would like to get out of the way before you cause a scene. There is a young, dark haired female in a white one-piece with navy polka dots leaning up against the beach wall down there reading Oblong Blank, who is registering positive to *Zeta*-E- methylamino -*A*-alanine-L. What are the odds? The device turned imperial. Yes, or no?"

"All right," Pinn quirked.

"Yes or no Pinn? This is a contract."

"It would be a lot less stressful for me Bruce, if you could ask politely."

"Deaththththththth," hissed the feral OyOyann as he stood. Turning away he said, "For the last time...."

"Yeththththththththth," Pinn liththththped.

Take Two

It was a splendid two-story house on a tree lined street in Twinkledale. A soon to be neglected rose garden lined the drive to the main entrance then doubled back next to itself with a small walkway between. Out the back, there was a grass tennis court with a teenage jacaranda growing in the center of it, a swimming pool to the right, lawn beyond, and a nunnery over the back fence. Once or twice in the morning, when he was staying in the second-floor western bedroom, Pinn saw some young girls in white uniforms with light blue aprons hanging sheets on long lines at the end of their yard.

Ming, Pinn's father, bought the house a year earlier with enough cash left over to do the addition he always wanted. His fame, thus, fluidity, was growing, and he wanted a laudable house in a respected suburb with its very own snooker hall.

A friend, a short, rotund, darkly dressed architect who liked to wear a wide brimmed hat and cape, designed a large games room to house Ming's snooker table ambition. His brother built it.

The old garage was demolished and replaced with a carport and a spacious hall, carpeted at one end, that extended out onto the tennis court almost to the jacaranda. There were large windows on three of the four walls so a complete view of the newly built carport, the pool, backyard, and tree lined fence on the left were highlighted.

Ming was chuffed with his arrangement and was keen to show off his new game's hall with a full-sized snooker table. He thought himself a better than competent player and owned a two-piece trexodynamically weighted cue, which he kept in a sturdy case.

Because he was a sporting professional, Ming knew other sporting professionals including some snooker players. He invited them around to try out his facility. One afternoon W.S., an Australian Snooker champion turned up. Another evening, H.L., a world billiards champion also visited. To twelve-year-old Pinn, both were very polite fellows wearing very black suits with very shiny shoes, very white shirts, and very bowed ties. W.S. wasn't particularly interested in the children, it was late anyway, but H.L. showed Pinn a trick or two.

Pinn arrived back in that time, on a Sunday, about forty-five minutes before he was shot by Gareth Spont, a lanky blond boy two years older.

Gareth's parents owned a cotton plantation near Emerald. They were inside talking to Ming about coaching and billeting their son for the summer.

Whenever Ming returned from an overseas trip, a more or less regular thing, he bought his wife and children presents. Two weeks earlier, upon his return from Canada, he presented pistols that shot pellets after a certain amount of pumping a lever below the barrel to his son and live-in younger nephew, Taylor. The boys shared space and sometimes played together. On this day, brandishing their new weapons the boys were playing massacreists in the backyard, mercilessly shooting flocks of dandelions, a squad of tree trunks, and a crow that squawked, "faaawk," and glared at the boy with one white eye as it flew off. When the Sponts turned up the boys were summoned to keep Gareth company while his parents made their pitch.

Being a country boy, Gareth was no stranger to guns, but he had never seen a pump-action pellet pistol before. He asked the boys if he could have a look at one. Taylor knew Pinn would never surrender his weapon, so he reluctantly volunteered his, along with a few pellets. Gareth took it, pocketed the pellets, waved the thing about a bit, asked if it was loaded and pulled the trigger.

Pinn buckled a little and clutched his left groin.

"Oops," said Gareth, turning toward the yard, pumping the weapon.

There was some ado in the following half hour before Gareth's parents re-emerged, at least where Taylor and Pinn were concerned. Neither knew what to do. Gareth had gone hunting. Pinn was not suffering a life-threatening injury. A pellet pierced his skin, not his favorite shorts. At first, there was no blood but when Pinn pulled at the cloth around the impact site the pellet popped out and bleeding ensued. Pinn was a bleeder. It was not an incident either boy wanted the Ming to learn about.

Pinn patched himself up with toilet paper and thin strips of masking tape fetched by Taylor.

They found Gareth leaning up against the Jacaranda casually shooting at a growing murder of crows.

Taylor, who the Ming sometimes referred to as a "Creeping Jesus," at the tender age of eleven could surprise. He quietly demanded Gareth give him back his gun. Gareth ignored him and kept pumping the pistol. He pointed to the bird he said he was going to plug between the eyes next. Taylor took Pinn's primed gun from Pinn's hand and shot the Jacaranda trunk three whiskers from Gareth's right ear. Gareth jumped, but shortly gathered himself and turned his weapon on Taylor.

Taylor calmly loaded and pumped his pistol, raised it, and shot again.

This time, whether intentionally or by fluke he shaved a single layer of skin from Gareth's left lobe.

Gareth fired but missed. He walked to the edge of the tennis court dabbing his ear and threw Taylor's gun into the pool. It didn't work after that.

The farewell was simple. Gareth was eager to go. His parents emerged from the back door. After a short run, he fell into step with them as they retreated up the driveway.

3.

"Nothing happened after that," said Pinn.

"Being present at the piercing of the skin was our only objective, said Bruce. "The portal is nine hours. Did you not enjoy it?"

Pinn said nothing.

"I thought the snooker tournament went well," Bruce pursued. "After the afternoon's events, it was a less eventful evening but then Ming thought sport and picked you out of Taylor and your sister to play snooker with after dinner. You were in particularly good form and won the first game 84, 27. Ming, an ungraceful loser, was unhappy but not yet disturbed. He challenged you again. You could not refuse. He chided you on your prissy break then brought up a snide issue. Martha, I think her name was. As he went for the black after sinking a lucky red, he berated a choice you supposedly made to which you uncharacteristically objected forcing him to miss the shot. You won that game 108, 21 and had to bunt the blue with the butt of your cue when it was thrown your way after you cleared it while pointing out Martha's obvious appeal. It put you 74 ahead. You had to duck the white also as it was returned to the dee for the third game, which didn't finish. It ended when livid Ming hurled the pink through the open window behind you after you'd sunk it for the third time. It knocked out Boner, the Great Dane cross, a full dog, who just happened to be trotting by."

"The piercing. Being present for the piercing," questioned Pinn, catching up?

"Yes, we expected with a little sleight of hand we could deliver the fix to a tenderer candidate at a more rampant developmental period. You may yet survive human."

"Survive?"

"Good grief, are you not capable of formulating a complete response?" Bruce rubbed his beard down a few times with his right hand. His palm was probably itchy.

Pinn waited.

"To us, to me, you are a species of interest. A developing being in the wrong place at the wrong time. A planetary cycle will wipe you out unless something is done. I have a plan but there is one more regression and we are yet to see if you can get a youngsters fix, affixed thereafter. How are Lilith and Belinda?"

"Lilith? Belinda?"

The god rolled his eyes. He wondered if consciousness was ever present in the species. "I say again, in a few more minutes you will be completely assimilated into your new circumstances and will remember nothing of the old."

"That's what you said last time," argued Pinn, "but that's not what happened. Right up until I was zapped again, I was still trying to figure out who was how and where what was."

"You are distracted by a certain awareness of our contract Pinn. That is all. There is no evidence to suggest any thought you ever had, or association you ever made, was ever not related to the world in which you existed then and exist now. Meridiana, for example, has always been in a chained relationship with a long haired, blonde, buff lad a few years younger than she who makes paintings of single white circles on large white canvases for a living.

"Who is Meridiana?"

"Exactly. Sixty-three minutes until your third regression Pinn. Think or thwim, either will work."

*

Pinn found himself at home pacing the pool deck.

"What's wrong," asked Lilith as he approached the end of his second lap. "Who have you been asked to kill this time?" She did not look up.

Pinn was unaware she was there. She was semi reclined on a banana bed in the shade by the bar. He stopped. She was wearing a dark two-piece costume, a dark, sheer, box coat and metallic grey Aah-Choo's with silver soles. She was reading.

Unable to formulate a response, Pinn resumed his pacing posture, did a little orientating hop, and started on another lap.

Lilith was unperturbed. She knew, if not at the end of the next lap, then definitely at the end of the one after, Pinn would erupt into a verbatious episode best left to run its course. It was hard to glean anything from such outbursts, but they were usually trying to get somewhere. The day was warm, there was nobody around, Margot had just met Axel in the book she had just begun. Lilith was open to the possibility of live amusement.

Unusually, at the end of lap five, when he finally did stop, there was no rant, no speech. Instead, a meek question was posed.

"Do you believe in....., have you heard of the OyOyann," asked Pinn, taking a seat on the edge of the banana bed opposite?

Good enough thought Lilith. She adjusted her bed to a more upright position, laid the book open on her lap and clasped her hands upon it. She turned to look directly at the man with whom she shared some of her life. His elbows were on his knees, his fingers were fidgeting amongst themselves, and he was contemplating his toes.

"Who hasn't?" was Lilith's response. She noticed he twinced. "They are probably just a clever invention of militant vegans or some other fanatical sway."

Pinn said nothing.

It was easy to dismiss Pinn's often expressed fantastical notions. His work involved a lot of guesswork and hope, so it was no wonder he sometimes claimed the household's white goods resonated in a frequency he understood, and returned his ability to dream and remember. Or that a potted orchid he named Vera whispered cryptic warnings, usually well in advance while he sipped his first cup of tea of the day. Pinn described Vera's predictions to Lilith retrospectively after fruition and he got it, but rarely explained from whence they came. He twinced. Pinn was relaxed in his whimsical world but quite the opposite in the world in which the rest of us live.

"Are you telling me Pinn, you were tapped by an OyOyann," said Lilith?

Pinn's reluctance to answer and the queer thing he did with his head indicated a yes to her.

"Am I in the first, second, or third out come," were Lilith's immediate thoughts? She was surprised when she realized she articulated them.

"The second," said Pinn.

"Should I be insulted?"

"I don't think so. I may have been manipulated but you are probably still the same you."

"Was that a sheep joke Pinn?"

They sat in silence for a few moments, each in their own world. Then, Lilith bucked up. "I'd be interested in meeting Bruce," she said. "How long until he turns up?"

"If he were to turn up," said Pinn, "it would be in the next thirty minutes, but I have to rendezvous with him at the highest, southern facing bench, at the park.

"Pervert."

"Indeed. Come for a walk with me Lilith, meet Bruce. We haven't walked in ages."

Putting the book to her left, Lilith swiveled, stood, and said she would be back before disappearing into a changing room close by.

When she emerged, she was wearing a classic white Adidas tracksuit left to flair, with a jack collar, and glossy white runners with burnt orange stripes. She looked stunning with all that red hair.

Pinn was wearing re-treaded Jesus Christ's with low viz socks, grey board shorts, and an even greyer, loose, polo shirt. He stood.

"What are you going to do," Lilith asked, linking her arm in his, marching him toward the door? "What point in your past are you going to choose to revisit this time and why?"

"Why?"

"Why?"

He told her he had absolutely no concept of any part of his so called, current life, and so had no idea what or where he was going to choose to revisit.

Lilith found confirmation of insult in Pinn's resoluteness but decided it was not intentional. She considered her options. She had visited Dr. Okazaki's site not three days before because Linda, Dean's brother's girlfriend, a tarotist of sorts who works out with her early in the morning three times a week at Jim's Gym reckoned she saw an OyOyann the other day at Coogee Bay buying a gross of charred rats at Blinky Bill's Pet Pentorium.

Lilith's interest was piqued from almost the first word on the good doctor's site. She spent a productive couple of hours there trying to form an opinion. In the end, she was undecided about the OyOyann objective. But something about the attitude of the snake from the Garden of Eden story as told by Dr. Okazaki, who uncharacteristically, romantically, suggested mythologized intricacies worth questing, twizzled Lilith's twick.

Pinn stopped at the threshold. Lilith clasped his shoulders with both hands and turned him to look at her. He dropped his eyes. She adjusted his collar. He felt her green gaze upon him. He sneaked a peak, then gesticulated with a defeated shrug. She pushed him out the door.

Tripping down the stairs with Lilith getting further and further behind, he said, "what I don't understand is Belinda."

"What," Lilith inflected unhearingly?

Pinn reached the bottom of the steps and turned to face her. She stopped where she was.

"What I don't understand is Belinda," he repeated.

"Belinda," questioned a terse Lilith, taking the six steps it took to join Pinn on the foot path two per syllable?

Pinn took a step back as she approached. He could feel her beating heart.

After a moment, he started up the escarpment toward the park. Lilith fell into step. She put her hands in her top pockets as if it was cold.

"It's a long story."

"I know you my sweet," said Lilith. "It will be what you make it."

"According to the OyOyann, I am not supposed to remember anything about anything and have a singular consciousness in my current life. But that is not the case. I know little of my current life yet remember a lot of things from my last two lives.

"The first, a choice made under duress, pointed toward maturity issues. The second involved a wound. Because I didn't know enough about what they were hoping for, Bruce offered to choose the next stop for me, then sent me back to my twelfth year and a specific moment.

"The wound?"

"Yes."

"Go on."

"He said, and I quote, 'we expected, with a little sleight of hand we could deliver the required fix to a tenderer candidate at a more rampant developmental period."

Pinn stopped and turned seaward. There was nothing to see but sea, maybe sky, and a red clay lip with sporadic green tufts. Lilith, still hands pocketed, tapped a foot a few steps beyond.

"The point of sleight of hand," he said, addressing the ocean before turning back and resuming his march, "was well before we met and since we have a daughter, wouldn't they know already if the trick took? Assuming their goal was a genetic thing."

"Are you accusing me of something Pinn?" asked Lilith, slowing to raise an eyebrow.

"Shortly, I have to step backward in time," said Pinn, "an action that could be my last, give or take nine hours tinkling in time past, and then a few minutes in the time we are in now. That's it, that's all there is for me if things go awry."

"Then get it right."

"Get what right? I don't know what's going on here. It sounds simple enough on paper but it's not in reality."

They were at the top of the hill, and they were facing each other. Pinn nodded in the direction of the OyOyann sitting on the bench further down the path. Lilith turned.

"Behold the god," Pinn said. "Fifteen minutes."

"Should we jog," asked Lilith?

Pinn smiled before he continued down the hill, slowing to a stroll, swinging his arms in time.

"I have two options," he said as Lilith slowed to join him, "consciousness, a choosing, or, capitulation, taking whatever is offered. The latter is most likely since the former seems to be missing."

"Don't kid yourself my love," said Lilith, "the former has always been missing. It hasn't stopped you before. Choose"

Pinn hmphed.

Then they were before the OyOyann.

Bruce stood.

"Bruce, Lilith, Lilith, Bruce," said Pinn, introducing the two. They shook hands. Bruce's wrist device was a luminous amber.

Lilith, suddenly, did not hide her agitation which had been privately festering unbeknownst to Pinn, since he first mentioned the OyOyann.

Addressing the god she said, "Do I exist, and if I do, will I continue to, or is it all over for me too when you do whatever you do to Pinn?"

Gods have the ability to do all sorts of things and this one on this occasion split into two people. One clone, for lack of a better description, dealt with Lilith, the other with Pinn, in a sort of momentary, bilateral world.

The OyOyann told Lilith she existed in more ways than she could possibly imagine, and she need not worry while telling Pinn in a different conversation a few steps away, if he didn't make his deadline there would be nothing he could do.

Lilith persisted. "A bit vague big guy," she said. "After you send Pinn wherever, will I become a non-existent? If not, what happens to me in, say, the next half hour?"

"She seems driven," said Pinn.

"You hadn't noticed," queried the OyOyann?

Bruce told Lilith she had a far better life ahead of her than she ever would have had, had she stayed with Pinn. This took her breath away at first, but she went on her way happily after Bruce revealed more details about her future then shoved her into it with a little push. She was given an extremely obedient big black dog with red upright ears on an exquisitely plaited de Sade leather leash, and an unearthly security detail of two, for life.

Bruce's device turned carmine.

"I am not Belinda's father then," stated Pinn, looking for confirmation. "If I was, this would be all over for me. Is that correct?"

"The immediate and subsequent answer Pinn is no. Belinda's father is Gristle Gore, Bellamy's younger brother. You were both at the same party and both did the deed with Lilith that night. He, up against the farthest wall in a cubicle in the ladies between mains and dessert, you flat on your back on a pink unicorn lilo in the pool long after most had left. The Gorster's seed took, and you married into it.

"It would not have been all over for you had Belinda been yours, but there is no need to get into that unless we must. Where to?"

"Belinda not being mine alleviates a few things," mused Pinn.

"Not now Pinn. Where to?"

Seconds passed. The OyOyann realized Pinn was in the same position he was in the last time. He let the seconds pass.

"No idea then Pinn," he asked eventually?

"None," said Pinn immediately.

The OyOyann let more seconds pass. "May I offer a suggestion," he asked?

"I am a captive, right," said Pinn? "Go for your life. Tell me."

"Captive is your word Pinn. I am not going there again. We are now, however many seconds to deadline. I understand you may be a little stressed, but let's keep the conversation neurosis free."

"Two hundred and thirty four seconds," said Pinn.

"You have forgotten your Suisse excursion."

A light went on when Bruce mentioned an incident at the post office.

"Are you talking about Catherine, Cat?"

"Yes, and her sister Michelle. If you were to simply rerun that play again but choose a better outcome, remembering there is no harm in being in the money, we can all move on. The fix is in place, and you did pretty well in that short period the first time around.

Pinn wandered over to the bench and sat. The OyOyann followed but stood behind.

"Do I become a Methuselah and have to watch over this thing for the next nine hundred years if I succeed," asked the Pinn?

"If you were to succeed, earthling, and not die in a spontaneous combustion event shortly after your next return, the answer is no. It is likely you will perish in fated time and some young upstart will take over your authority.

"Twenty-seven seconds Pinn."

"I cede," Pinn uttered, "but under one condition. If I fail, I still get to understand."

"Good luck with that," the god offered as Pinn was engaged.

Third Time Lucky

Pinn met Catherine at the Picnic Bay Hotel, Magnetic Island. She was a backpacker. They were about the same age. She told him, after the event, she thought him a bit meek and wouldn't have entertained his approach at all had she not witnessed the glass duel a few nights earlier at the pool table end of the completely tiled bar room. They spent a few days together, then she had to fly home. She said she would come back after she sorted a couple of things out. Two months later she returned. By that time Pinn had relocated to Sydney and was living at Kings Cross in a ground floor apartment across the lane from the Hyatt Hotel. He was finalizing his schooling at a nearby university. This too was a brief encounter for the pair. Three days into a twenty one day visit, after a big day out, Cat presented an ultimatum to Pinn, and returned home the following day.

The ultimatum was simple: "Follow me."

A few weeks later, after submitting his thesis, Pinn did.

Pre OyOyann, Pinn's visit to Vevey, Switzerland lasted three months and during that time he impregnated Cat as well as her sister Michelle, but when faced with dealing with it opted out for a neat sum. The short option the OyOyann offered.

Catherine was the more serious second daughter of Gorm and Nellie Blingcrowd, nee Calvin, the family money. The first daughter, Michelle was a less serious girl and for that, better liked. She was blonde haired, blue eyed and physically unwanting. Unlike her plainer and sportier younger sister, she was more socially orientated. One unlucky day in the summer of her eighteenth year and her sister's seventeenth, the girls were struck down as they crossed the road after lunching with friends at a trattoria on Rue de la Madeleine by a Vesper driven by a jealous ex of the older girl. Both suffered a number of minor fractures and some grazing but unexplainably, thereafter, Michelle demonstrated symptoms of paraplegia for which doctors could find no physical cause and thus, could not cure. Upon her release from hospital, she was confined to a wheelchair.

As an outpatient, in the months that followed, Michelle underwent a number of psychiatric evaluations and for a while participated in physiotherapy programs designed to help her get back on her feet. Nothing worked. The only thing doctors found was their mother's older brother Sven had put her across his knee and given her a sound spanking for letting the pigs out for the third day in a row when she was twelve. The girls had spent the summer at his farm while their parents visited the Americas, partly for pleasure, partly for business. In the end it, was decided by Dr. Hang Hong, the lead specialist on Michelle's medical team, an enthusiastic spanking by a sour uncle was hardly likely to trigger lower body motorlessness six years later after a minor accident. A solution was abandoned by all except Cat.

Curiously, Michelle did not seem all that put out by her predicament which became a frustration for Cat who, rather than harboring sibling rivalry, idolized her sister and could not understand her complacency about her state.

Gorm had the garden house, a single-story house further down the grounds converted into suitable lodgings for Michelle's condition. She loved it. Gorm's renovations made it a big garden house with a recreation wing and a heated pool. It overlooked a green and pristine valley and had a view of Lake Geneva in the distance. Cat moved in with her sister. With the help of Gustaf, Michelle's chauffeur, a neat, svelte Svede whose resemblance to Michelle was uncanny, and Greta, the maid, Catherine and Michelle resumed their lives. Cat fussed to Michelle's acquiescence. Gustaf lived in a cottage a whistle away.

*

Pinn didn't say he was coming and rang Cat from the jetty upon arrival. He did the tourist thing and took the ferry across the lake. It was Autumn and not so busy. Catherine was out of town. She was unhappy with the surprise but got Gustaf to pick Pinn up.

The girls' world was full of money. It was a foreign world to Pinn, which was all too obvious to the guys and gals of Cat's circle. In the beginning, he got away with being an odd Aussie hick.

Out of his depth, Pinn did what he always did. Hid. At the time of his arrival, the Baldwin twins were occupying the guest quarters in the garden house. They had been there since Cat's twenty first birthday celebrations a week earlier so Pinn was assigned to Gustaf's guest room. It was small but comfortable. Pinn found Gustaf to be an odd fellow with remarkable focus and stringent ways. He also found him to be exceedingly generous in that he gave Pinn use of his private automobile, a small Fiat 600, while he was in residence.

Pinn was grateful and nipped here and there locally in it.

Catherine had commitments she could not get out of at the time and admonished Pinn for not informing her of his pending arrival.

Three days later and one before he thought he might cut his losses and go home, Pinn found Michelle expecting him as he wandered out of the Chateau de l'Aile just after noon.

Gustaf was waiting near the entrance as Pinn exited the building. He shepherded him toward a small grass way by the lake where Michelle was talking to her sister on the phone.

Pinn waited. Walked away a little as the conversation went on.

Pinn was not afraid of admitting to personal bigotries. He reckoned most folks had them. There were many in his case; fat people, skinny people, those with skin problems, aggression, toothlessness, smiles, age, testosterone, tattoos, shortness, height, deformity, sickness, and the list goes on. Despite Michelle ticking a number of those boxes, she still held Pinn's interest. She was angelically beautiful and didn't seem to fit into the imposed confinement.

Gustaf, quite the beauty himself with that flush physique and wavy blond curves, indicated with a click of his heels and a nod that Michelle was free. Pinn turned.

Michelle told Pinn Catherine was still in Beirut and would be for the next four days and that the Baldwin twins had gone home so the guest rooms were vacant.

Gustaf, unlike Pinn, was used to the weight of Michelle's words. He said he would drive the Fiat back to the estate, which left Pinn to awkwardly chauffeur Michelle home.

That afternoon Pinn moved into the guest quarters in the garden house and Gustaf applied for emergency leave. His father was ailing he said, and he was. He died the following day.

Alone in the garden house, Pinn and Michelle incubated like new life. Duties, relating to Michelle's care, usually performed by Gustaf or Catherine if she were home, Pinn performed in their absence. He found them incredibly intimate and arousing. The slinkiness into which the pair slank was affirmative. To Pinn, Michelle was the goddess of the chariot, impossible to ignore. By the dawn of the second day, randy Pinn had seeded her. She was a gift, a fantasy, everything, and Pinn thought himself mighty. She reckoned a few more treatments and she could be cured.

The usually busy house had only one visitor during Cat's absence, Gorm, who turned up early one Sunday morning after hearing from Gary, the gate guy, a little after 2:00 am, when he returned after a few days away, none of the usual folks had been through to see Michelle since Pinn moved into the house. He found Pinn lapping freestyle in the pool. He took a seat, lit a cigarette. It was a lovely morning.

When Pinn launched himself from the water onto the pool deck in a single movement in that cute, yellow cossie after he had done his lap schedule, Gorm applauded. Pinn, who didn't realize he was there, went for his towel.

Greta had been watching the two from the kitchen window since she arrived for work fifteen minutes earlier. She woke Michelle when she thought Pinn may need help. She took coffee and pastries to a small table between the two as Michelle rolled out onto the patio on her father's side.

The favorite daughter convinced Gorm Pinn was just babysitting until Cat came back, adding, it was fortunate he just happened to be visiting in the light of Gustaf's sudden unavailability.

It was obvious to Pinn, wearing a team paranoid tracksuit, Michelle had a way with her father.

Soon after Gorm's visit, Pinn began to wonder how things might play out when Cat returned home. He spoke to Michelle about it. She advised him to forget the last three, almost four days completely and go on as if nothing happened. Gustaf had returned and was ready to resume his post.

The advice was not what Pinn expected. He couldn't and didn't forget but forged on regardless.

It was not until late on the third day after her return that Catherine became with child.

No one knew the sisters had been fertilized at that point. Cat remained busy and was often away. Pinn was spending time at Glenst Yng and took over some of Gustaf's duties where Michelle's care was concerned. Heaven.

Cat found out first. She had had a little more flatulence than usual as she worked out at the gym one morning and took herself off to the doctor after the session for a check-up. A precautionary measure. It had been a while. The doctor performed all the usual tests and ten minutes later came back with a diagnosis of pregnancy.

The look on Catherine's face after being presented with the diagnosis prompted the doctor to excuse his young nurse, lower his voice, and state that while this particular clinic did not perform abortions, he did have another that did and could provide a referral if necessary. Cat left without saying a word and decided before getting into her car for the drive home she would not tell a soul.

Two weeks later while undergoing her normal quarterly physical it was discovered Michelle was also with child. This was not reported to Michelle directly but rather to her father. Cripples are often regarded as being cripple in more ways than one.

Gorm confided in Catherine since Nellie advised it. She was in St. Petersburg.

Catherine didn't seem surprised which made Gorm even more uneasy. However, for his second daughter, against his better judgement, Gorm wanted to have the upstart killed there and then, he allowed Catharine's request for a three-day moratorium. Her mother would be back by then and, on second thoughts thought, a straight slaying might be too good for the incubus.

When Cat told Pinn she was pregnant, Michelle was the first to congratulate her. The three were fondueing Bombay duck, scampi, and celery poolside at about 6 pm. It was cool. Catherine declined the wine and drank spritz. They were the only three in the house besides security measures.

From Catherine's announcement, the evening was like falling down the rabbit hole for Pinn. He woke feeling unsettled the next morning, still in the same chair, with fairy tale memories of the night before. In the beginning, he was the reluctant but honest father to be. Catherine revealed Michelle was also pregnant, so then he became the despicable philanderer. In the light of the first revelation, Michelle's pregnancy was only a semi surprise to Pinn, but not so to Michelle. She was overjoyed and almost jumped out of her chair. Pinn didn't know who to turn to. The girls did some sort of sister thing for a misty amount of time and after that, Pinn was singularly unpresent. He wondered if something had been put in his drink. Across a glowing round table, he answered questions asked by Cat, then Michelle, then both in unison, with a single grunt. There was incense, sitars played, and at one point Catherine sprang from her seat and did a little jig. It seemed like a ritual and Pinn felt like he was selling his soul. For what exactly, he didn't know.

Pinn made his way to the kitchen where Cat was blending a dark concoction which the girls subsequently drank through thick straws. She offered some to Pinn, who declined. It smelt like arse and looked like sump oil.

A big day lay ahead. The moratorium ended at noon. Nellie and Gorm were expecting everyone on the southern terrace of the main house at 5 pm.

Catherine presented her plan while Pinn munched on cornflakes and milk topped with banana, chocolate syrup, blueberries, raspberries, and more sugar. Sometimes Michelle added a little extra clarification and touched his knee. The plan was long and detailed but did not include how Pinn might deal with the parent's reaction to both daughters being suddenly sired, Gorm's word.

At face value, Pinn would be Catherine's. After that, she and her sister had an abstract sharing system in place, not unlike what was already going on. Supposedly, temporarily, until Michelle found her feet.

Notwithstanding the ritual, Pinn was surprised the girls thought him a keeper. The boys they already knew were much more in tune with it all, and rich to the last.

So here we are, flatly, at Pinn's last time warp.

*

Pinn slept through the first three hours of his third return. Against the rules, the OyOyann picked his arrival time. "Relax," said Bruce," it will be all right."

When Pinn woke, but for himself, the garden house was empty.

Expecting the girls to return and take him up to the main house for the meeting, Pinn lolled around outside drinking coffee and eating yellow iced doughnuts until a storm began rolling in. It darkened, a gentle pitter patter rain started up, and there was a low rumble in the distance.

By 4:56 pm, Pinn realized no one was coming for him and he would have to make it up to the house of his own volition. The rain had hardened by then and the rumble of thunder had grown and tightened. He witnessed an atmospheric flash that turned the landscape into a negative as he looked down the valley. When he opened the door to leave, there was a clap of thunder so tumultuous he could feel his diaphragm contract.

The main house was three hundred meters up a sloping cobblestone drive, and Pinn's only choice was to walk it or run it. The rain continued to get heavier. The lightning became more fractious and crackled in ripples, spreading tentacles all over before a deafening clap finished the take.

Pinn started up the hill at a good walking pace but soon broke into a jog. He did not try to protect himself from the rain. He was wearing long dark shorts, a floppy dark T-shirt that said Watt? in white, and some unsuitably fine moccasins he found at the front door. Except for the shoes he looked like he was off to shoot a few hoops. The electrics began to concern him.

Twenty meters from the house, Pinn's short, wet hair stood on end. Fretful, Pinn put what energy he could muster into his legs and sprinted toward the building.

More than several minutes later he awoke flat on his back at the foot of the front entrance to the main house. Gustaf turned up, told Pinn he was late in that way of his, didn't help him get to his feet, but when Pinn did, led him through the corridors to the southern terrace by the light of a lantern.

Entering the southern terrace through the house one walks between a pair of good sized, five legged, Lamassu.

"So nice of you to finally join us," Gorm shouted from across the way, raising his glass. A flash and a good crack of thunder followed.

Despite his drenched and dripping state, as things fell, Pinn didn't look too bad. The moccasins helped. He was slim, had good posture and teeth. His hair was short, his gaze was steady and in looks rated about a twelve on the Cantoscatt scale.

Gorm and the girls were dressed formally, Gorm in black, the girls in white. Pinn could not see Nellie. She was behind and left. Approaching. She had ducked out to see if anyone had seen Pinn. She, in fact, found him unconscious at the doorstep and summoned Gustaf.

Linking her arm in his, but not moving him on, Nellie said, "I like the drenched look Pinn, but next time see if you can do it without the water."

She smelt of purple hyacinth. Pinn sort of bowed. He had only seen, but not met Nellie, once before. She unlinked herself from his arm and stepped back.

Gorm and the girls turned their attention back to themselves.

"Snake tells me you are a binotronic pinch," said Nellie.

Pinn momentarily made eye contact but didn't respond.

"Snake also tells me, "she went on, putting herself into profile like an Egyptian hieroglyph, "you fixed a glitch in our service software by adding a simple virus."

"My virus is harvesting your data Mrs. Blingcrowd, so I, thank you."

"For the moment, call me Nellie, Pinn," she said, "but who knows, you may be calling me mummy soon. Would you like that?"

Nellie was quite a presence. She was tall, slim, and shapely, and it was not hard to tell from whom her daughters inherited their charms. Gorm was squarer and closer to the ground. Pinn had been told Nellie liked to dress dramatically from time to time and sometimes smoked a cigarette through a long holder. On this night she wore a simple white chin to floor linen and chiffon sheath with a jagged titanium nonagonal hasp accentuating her bust.

Pinn remained silent.

"I would," she said, smiling, linking her arm through his again, "but perhaps not for the reasons you may be thinking."

Pinn allowed Nellie to lead him from the room. Gustaf went ahead holding a lantern. At the Lamassu's tails, Gustaf handed the lantern to Pinn and went back. Nellie thanked him and steered Pinn left.

"So," began Nellie, adding a surprise skip to her step which dragged the lad along briefly, "who do you prefer? Michelle, or Catherine? This is no time to be silent boy."

"Said Merdwyn to Merkin," responded Pinn drily.

"Oh dear, you're one of them," Nellie tished. "How disappointing. Truth be told, I don't care who you prefer. The girls will work it out and Gorm will help them whether you like it or not. My interest, for the moment, lies in your interest.

"For the last few weeks, you have spent a certain amount of time working on a project of your own in a corner of our Glenst Yng facility. This came about because you had a conversation with Snake at some party a few days after you arrived. He said you were obviously not as familiar as the rest of the group with the drinks and the drugs and behaved overly friendly because of it, but you remained surprisingly coherent for much of the night.

"Late in the evening or early in the morning, Snake was not specific, you found yourselves in conversation. You have a challenging way according to Snake. I am yet to see it. Anyway, you produced a small crude box, which you put on the table. You told Snake that, except where you were concerned, the box could tell the holder the first nine words a person approached or who approaches will utter nine seconds before they utter it, correctly, ninety six percent of the time. You said it was a simple device dependent more on feeling the variables in an environmental moment but tapped into enough systems could predict, depending on the strength of the mathematics, the future in almost absoluteness."

"I said that," Pinn questioned?

"No, that's what I got from Snake's story," said Nell. "But it was on the strength of your little machine, which tested well, even with robots, that you were left alone to do as you pleased. We had hoped you would eventually work with us so we could offer you a job. But you knocked up a few more boxes, one of which I have, thank you, and except for the <blackscroll> sends/ issue fixed only recently you worked almost entirely alone and kept off the network. Snake remains unsure how your box works. He suspects the device receives rather than processes information."

"He is wrong," said Pinn.

"Which brings me to one of the reasons we are here on this porch in this unsettling storm. I have a proposal."

The sky winked.

"Shall we sit?"

Nellie indicated a table in an open corner with booth seats. Pinn was relieved to have somewhere to put the lamp. They sat opposite. Gustaf turned up with a tray of refreshments, a pitcher of martinis, chilled glasses, stuffed olives, whole red chilies, Camembert, crackers, plump dried apricots, and seedless green grapes.

After thirty minutes, two martinis, and a little apricot and cheese, Pinn agreed to Nellie's proposal, including the caveat that he marry one of her daughters. Pinn signed some pages surreptitiously delivered by Gustaf with the refreshments. They toasted and sat back. A cigarette would have been nice.

"Now you must face Gorm," said Nellie after a while, beginning to wriggle out of her seat. "Let's hope the girls have been at work. It will have peeved Gorm that I stole you away. I didn't tell him of my plan so he will be furious when he finds out, if he has not already guessed, but not with me." She picked up the lamp. After you, she gestured.

The storm clapped excessively Pinn thought as they re-entered the southern terrace, and there was so much strobing light he feared he would have a seizure. At the end of the table, Cat, in profile, was bent over a magazine layout she and Michelle were scrutinizing. One hand on the table, one hand on a hip which she reversed as Pinn and Nellie reappeared. Was her belly beginning to show Pinn wondered?

Gorm stood. Drink in hand he strode toward Nellie and Pinn, glaring at Nellie, extending a hand to Pinn when he was close enough. Gustaf took the lantern from Nellie. Pinn took Gorm's hand. It was firm, very firm. Gorm pulled Pinn in as if in a dance, threw his arm, glass in hand, over Pinn's shoulders, and spun him toward a less lit and less sheltered part of the terrace without spilling a drop. They walked hip to hip briefly before Gorm let go.

"Catherine told me her plan," Gorm began when they reached his preferred field of battle, a bar. This one by the pool was barely under cover. "What do you think?"

Gustaf appeared again, put a corked bottle of honey bourbon, a modest bucket of ice, the remains of the pitcher of martini, and a clean glass for Pinn on the bar, and left.

"The box you gave Snake," Gorm continued, producing it, "says you are about to say, Locklessness reeks tweezer shapes tongue tied twice azure Wednesday."

"I apologize, sir," said Pinn, "I am not recognizable to the box and it has a bit of waywardness about it yet. At the moment, the machinery is still easily blocked or hoodwinked. Let me show you. May I have it?"

Gorm passed the device to Pinn. Pinn flipped it. The small monitor ticker taped the words, you're an idiot if you think Nellie was fooled.

"You're an idiot if you think Nellie was fooled Pinn," said Gorm. "Your little device works in certain controlled conditions. Whoopee." Eyes were raised along with an accompanying right handed index twirl.

Pinn held the device up so Gorm could see the scrolling words. Pinn reset the machine. Gorm was unimpressed and temporarily remained silent. Shortly, the machine produced another string which Gorm in turn duplicated. After showing the second string to Gorm, Pinn lobbed the device into the pool with a deft Frisbee style stroke. He nodded slightly as it plopped into the water. He took a sip of martini.

From then on, Gorm just wanted to shoot Pinn or have Gainlee, head of his security, come and do it for him.

Pinn felt the animosity.

"What did you and Nell talk about," asked Gorm, trying out a wandering falsetto?

After pondering, Pinn began, "The discussion was predicated on a certain abstract in Nellie's fanciful..... "

"Everything is," interrupted Gorm. "What did you specifically talk about?"

More pondering. "In a nutshell, I was offered and accepted a lifetime of affluence for two commitments."

"Which were?"

"I marry one or both of your daughters."

"And the other?"

"I continue to work on my dark side."

"Getting tired of this Pinn," growled Gorm. "Spit it out boy, what exactly did Nell give you?"

"And there it is," said Nellie. She had joined the girls at the table but continued standing. All were looking at the boys in the semi darkness. "He just asked Pinn what I gave him."

"And you know that how mother," challenged Cat, "the rain is pelting down and I can barely hear you?"

She noticed the little black box in her mother's shadowed hand. Everybody was feeling the pinch. Then a dawning thought. Catherine took a step back, maybe two, "What did you offer him mother? How much does it cost to sell your daughters?"

"Ohoo, is that a dummy spit Cat," asked Nellie, dropping the device onto the table? "Tutt, Tutt. You are not sold yet. You are big girls now. You have to agree to it first."

Catherine squirmed. Michelle seemed content.

"My business with Pinn relates to his toy, that toy," she said pointing at it on the table.

"What did you give him mother," persisted Cat?

"The possibility of entering an unexplored frontier at whose door he is already knocking and a road that will make him a god to all who follow."

"What did you give him mother," both girls asked together with insistence?

Nellie sat. Catherine pulled the chair out for her.

"Don't make this about me girls," said Nell. "You are the one who brought him here Catherine. And you, Michelle, were not backward in coming forward when he did get here. Fate has it he just happens to be working on something we have only dreamed of being able to produce."

"So, you gave him what, mother?" Catherine drilled.

Nellie took a deep breath, feigned a sigh, then said in a sure voice, "A full partnership in the family enterprise at root level. On paper, he will have been adopted by my parents."

While the girls were choking on that, Nellie watched Gorm stagger toward her. She wasn't sure he'd make it. He looked like he was about to have a heart attack. She stood.

Gorm was on his knees by the time he reached Nell. He raised his arms and placed his hands together above his head as if in prayer. He said nothing. There was a grimace on his face and you could see tears running down the corners of his squinted eyes.

"Get up," said Nellie, "it's not the first time someone has married a relative or even two of them. Let your heart rest in the fact this is not about blood; it's about money."

"That makes me feel so much better," said Gorm heaving himself onto his feet then staggering back a little, "when that upstart signs whatever papers....."

"He already has," said Nell.

The debilitating oscillation that resonated through Gorm's physicalness at that point is impossible to describe. It took several minutes for the phenomena to wash through him. When he recovered, he did so left faced.

"Leaving money out of it," he started, "though that bum, that wandering baculum is now the two hundred and twenty fifth richest man in the world...."

"Good," quipped Nellie. "You wouldn't want your daughters marrying a pauper, would you?"

"No," gloomed Gorm, "marrying a rich uncle is so much better."

Gorm growled again lowly and longly. He walked down the table to where Gustaf had placed a drink. He sat. The girls seemed okay. There was animation between them. It momentarily eased Gorm's angst.

Eventually, everybody was seated at the table, Nellie at the head. On her left, three chairs down, Gorm. On her right, Catherine, Michelle, a space, then Pinn.

The sisters thought it a bit cavalier of Pinn to make a commitment to marry one of them without asking either. Catherine also questioned the apparent needs of a business and whether ingesting Pinn into it using flesh and money was not a sordid grab that had nothing to do with them. That got a guffaw from Gorm.

The storm mooded the terrace. It provided a comforting white noise most of the time but there was occasional belligerence and aggression.

Details were worked out.

Catherine, Michelle and Pinn would remain living in the garden house for the foreseeable future. Even after the wedding.

There was discussion come argument about Pinn's role in the business. Mostly between Nellie and Gorm though Pinn, unwisely, opened his mouth once.

Synchronized with a good flash of lightning, a light bulb flickered on above embattled Gorm's head. Addressing Pinn, he asked, "Is love present? Love. You know. That thing usually evident between couples committing to marriage. I've heard no talk of it. Do you love my daughters?"

Over the period of discussion there had been movement. Pinn got up to get another martini for himself and San Pellegrino for the girls before Gustaf could do it. Drink wise, Nellie was happy, Gorm was right.

Michelle accompanied Pinn when he went to the bar then steered him back to a seat beside Catherine. Gustaf had rearranged the chairs so that Pinn could sit between the two girls.

When Gorm brought up love, Pinn was holding Michelle's and Catherine's hand under the table like a fourteen-year-old.

Both let go and turned to face him hipping their free hand.

Pinn, disappeared. Time was up.

4.

Pinn was sitting on a bench, north of the quay, looking out over the lake, when he was joined by a fellow dressed as a lumberjack who, he learnt later, was OyOyann. His name was Bruce. Pinn pretended he was still alone.

Shortly Bruce spoke. "Congratulations," he said.

Pinn did not respond.

It was a fine autumn morning, still brisk. Neither moved much on the bench. Both looked lakeward, legs outstretched, hands pocketed in jeans.

"You survived," said the OyOyann. "Let's stroll?"

Pinn was reluctant but complied.

"I am going to describe a complicated scenario Pinn," said the OyOyann as they set off at a hands repocketed pace. "I will be brief, so pay attention."

"Emerging from the apparition after Mar's conjunction with the sun around 2026, it will become apparent that Venus, for whatever reason, has begun to behave erratically regarding its orbit. Then at the end of April 2029 when the sun, Mercury, and Saturn are supposed to align with Venus, a further change to her orbit occurs which will bring her into collision with Earth two years later. February 2031. More an atmospheric graze than a collision, really, but catastrophic enough for you guys. We need you to build an ark, Pinn."

The boys walked on.

Assuming anything you are saying makes sense, or will actually eventuate Bruce," said Pinn, "that's a pretty big ask, don't you think?"

Bruce waggled his head in response and pitched a wavering C nasally.

"Let me summarize," said Pinn. "After being hijacked on the dubious claim I carry a gene acronymed ZEAL, I was impelled to participate in a time, relationship, selection process. Now, having passed on to the next level, I am compelled to manage some sort of plan you lot, whoever you are, have come up with to deal with this supposedly, foreseeable devastation. And I am doing it to serve your needs."

"Not bad Pinn, but the plan to succeed will be yours."

They stopped. The OyOyann took a small matt black toothpick sized thing on what looked like a key ring from his pocket and handed it to Pinn.

"Let *me* summarize," said Bruce. "In the blink of an eye you have gone from a thirty-seven-year-old with a wife and family, living an inconspicuous life near a southern Sydney beach in Australia, to being a player. You are one of the richest men in the world. You have skin in the game. And now, because of your lineage, you have been given the opportunity to save yourself, your family, a few other things for us, and whatever else you can manage."

"What's this," Pinn asked holding up the toothpick?

"When I said build an ark, Pinn, I did not necessarily mean employ an arkwright and assemble a menagerie. If you had enough money, and you almost do, you could buy Egypt. There is a perfectly sound survival complex already built on the Giza Plateau. It would need a little cleaning up but it's still operational. However, with that option off the table, you have some work ahead of you.

"The Venus variation will be picked up in the usual way by the relevant agencies on Earth in 2026. When it is confirmed there will be a collision, two years after the conjunction, early in 2029, five years from now, some of the money will think to abandon the planet and go into space. Some will be ready for it and may succeed. You, on the other hand, Pinn, must stay.

"The last time a planetary disturbance happened to the Earth, five, almost six thousand years ago, we were visiting Skotosia for the Mardi Gras season and underestimated certain aspects of the phenomena. We think we have a better handle on it now. It, the object is a key. You will find it helpful."

He took it from Pinn, held it in his right hand, with thumb and fools' finger, and raised it until it poofed like a flashbulb of old.

"You're activated," he said handing it back to Pinn. "Engineer your survival."

"Or what?"

"Miss out on all the fun."

"If what you are saying comes true, the more or less instantaneous death of quite a few folks globally, one of which could be me, fun is not the noun that comes to mind."

"Or die carelessly."

Bruce feigned exasperation.

"Look," he said, "it might not be easy but it's doable. Your key can confirm it - the object just activated. It, firstly, is an identifier, but also in a sort of AI Yahweh, a knower of all, the alpha and the omega."

"An Identifier?"

"Yes, since you now qualify, our scribes need to be able to record what you do or do not achieve."

"In cuneiform, on tablets?"

"When you were twelve, we applied the chemical fix. Soon after you turned eighteen, you stopped talking about your theories because you sounded like a lunatic, even to yourself. But you still went on to develop the Box. That, you will find, morphs into a lucrative fortune telling app you call, ReadMe. Money and resources are almost no object. Live or die, it's up to you.

"I can't tell you more about the key, Pinn, you will have to work that out for yourself. I'm done here. I'll leave you to it. May your insights keep you erect, may your erectness give you measure, may your strength equal it.

Part Two

ReadMe

The story continues on from almost a year after Pinn's arrival at his third regression. With the shift of focus from what he was to what he became, there is a history to convey which wasn't available before. Before he was a middle manager in the advertising department of a daily newspaper. Not an odds-on choice for a global catastrophe hero. However, as a wealthy computer geek and an amateur physicislibrieist with oodles of family money, two wives, a concubine and five children, well..., we'll see. But not in this part.

Below is a whistle stop excursion through Pinn's history from 2009 to Saturday, October 12, 2024.

*

Pinn, Michelle, and Catherine married toward the end of January 2009 at a quaint castle just outside Bärg, Liechtenstein. It was a small affair attended mostly by family but a half a dozen others were invited. The nuptials were uniqueish. The ritual was recognized. The Ming couldn't make it, but Shirley and Delores could. Both babies had been born by then. Justine to Michelle, December 12, 2008, and Izabella to Catherine, nine days later.

A nannie named Renée was engaged. Another svelte Svede.

Immediately after the wedding, Pinn embarked on a garden house expansion project. He approached Gorm for permission. He loved the estate. After haggling a little upon seeing the plans, mostly about the so-called workstation, Gorm and Nellie approved the new buildings as long as Pinn paid all construction costs and built a temporary access road to minimize their inconvenience.

A substantial children's wing was stepped to the garden house. A little further down the drive, even more spacious guest housing was built. But the jewel in the crown of the expansion was Pinn's workstation, which he called, Cubus. A thirty six meter corical with a clear domed lid. It looked like that from the garden house but from the main house further up the hill, when it was not in stealth mode, which it often was, it looked more like a mottled green, razeed sphere.

It seemed to float between the main house and the garden house and had its own carpark. That too had a stealth mode. It sat atop a sort of docking station, which connected to the garden house via an arcade three stories below. A Saturn wing frame held it in place and provided a ramp to the drive.

Catherine tried to delegate a little and travel less, so by the time construction was completed, the family were living in a modestly obscene amount of space with perfect alpine views. Gustaf and Greta became a couple and Greta moved into Gustaf's cottage.

One day Renée came home with a dog. He was a big fellow, young and goofy but Anubic at rest. She said he could talk. She said she hadn't heard him talk yet but the lady who gave him to her assured her he could. She said his name was Gene.

Pinn kept to himself, which Gorm admired. They met occasionally and talked less. For Gorm, while the status was no longer quite quo, he was happy enough.

2.

ReadMe, Pinn's fortune-telling app's fortunes developed slowly.

Pinn didn't know where the information that enabled him to build the first box came from. It was simply in his head on the day he turned eighteen. It was complicated and difficult to assimilate, but when he did assimilate it, he considered it a gift. Sort of like, give me one free miracle and I will create the rest.

It started with presence. Being there.

The original box sampled the chemical wash of an individual as it was held by the user and could, by monitoring outside influential chemistry at the same time, number future possibilities. All Pinn did was trick a fuzzy touch to the system to get predictionettes. Knowing something of the chemical saturation contained in any given body at any given moment, and those reacting to it in its immediate orbit, without any added electronic input whatsoever, turned out to be extraordinarily cutch.

Pinn built a virtual universe. He was given the basement of the Glenst Yng facility, about fifty square meters of space. It took nine months to assemble and configure and during that time Pinn installed an underground cable to Cubus, a trunk, to save himself the commute.

Pinn's reckoning was; to create an environment in which they could positively forecast future events, all they had to do was pick a starting point, now, tomorrow, the day after, whenever (April 31, 2010: Global Daze's minutes), and from that day onward, collect every plankobyte of data they could lay their hands on. Come up with a way to store and catalog it and have a system for swift and intuitive retrieval.

"We will never know everything, because we started in the middle of something else but in our creation, our modest black hole," said Pinn, "we have probably got some power. We should be able to predict almost any future up to a point."

"Providing we can fix the measurement problem," said Snake.

*

Six months later they were doing well on the first part, but not very on the second and third until, one night, Snake stumbled upon 217924 or, Brix as it came to be known, in the bargain basement of a hacker's hut in the burgeoning dark web. Software from the eighties by one Garhill Grenslaw. Its computing was succinctly simple, but its treat was that it solved a significant storage issue with a uniqueness still secreted today. Pinn, personally, bought the copyright.

Once Snake got Brix organized to handle Pinn's Creation software, all that was left was to get the Box to join the party, so to speak. The plan was to have each source hit the same single point in time bringing with it the data it had – Creation; the road traveled, Brix; statistics, the Box; the environment. From there, they believed they could construct a prediction longer than nine words. They didn't know how yet, but they were working on it.

Around then, Pinn played from time to time, N.O.L.F., a first-person PC spy game from the '90's, set in the '60's. He was fond of Ria Mone, one of the characters. She was a fierce and physical female.

The way the game dealt with certain decisions astonished Pinn. He couldn't pinpoint how they were doing it. It was discovered later by Snake, after, again, Pinn acquired the rights to the software, at certain impasses the algorithm called by the handler to deal with the problem, finished with open plugs. It meant the program was getting the information it needed to close the argument from outside of itself.

Pinn worked alone in Cubus. One day he decided he needed a virtual personal assistant. For amusement, he chose to fashion her after Ria from N.O.L.F. But called her Ramone. Most of his clerical or personal assistant tasks were handled by Sarah at Glenst Yng. She was somebody's sister's girlfriend. She was not unqualified for the position, but she was cold. Fierce hair, probably a Pisces. Before Snake assigned her to Pinn's whims, she was working with a team developing snorkel indices. A protocol used with a whistling device and earpiece which, after a little practice, allowed the operator to converse with dolphins, in dolphin.

Pinn found some basic coding for a personal assistant and went to work. Twelve days later Ramone was born aged twenty something. Pinn incorporated the open plugs of her namesake and added an, as yet, unstabilized, artificial intelligence package he had been tinkering together.

Her arrival sparked the beginning of what was to become ReadMe.

3.

On day nine of Ramone's development, Pinn experienced an epiphany. He told nobody. A bright white light appeared in the morning soon after he arrived for work which drew him toward it. At first, he thought he had somehow died and the light would present a synopsis of his spiritless existence, but when, instead, it began sprouting about spot squatters in a vacuum and their fondness for quasiness, there was transcendence. Light off, light on. It was a threshold, a moving number in the Gloxomony Outcome. Meaningless to you or I.

Pinn kept Ramone on the Cubus array. At first, her clumsy interactions gave Pinn amusement. Pinn tweaked her here and there and she learnt quickly, too quickly. He soon felt like smoking a cigarette after a good tweaking.

It took a few months before Pinn tested Ramone on other folks. They all knew she was there. The girls especially. Pinn was spending long hours at Cubus. One afternoon when Snake dropped in to put some coins in the fountain about where the current difficulty lay in his Camelot, Pinn decided to include Ramone in the conversation. "Snake, Ramone," Pinn spoke as Snake entered through the front doors. "Ramone, Snake."

"Pleased to meet you," Ramone responded.

Snake was pleased to meet her too but got on with it as was his way.

According to Snake the Creation package and Brix worked like vegemite on toast but the Box refused to be the avocado. So far, no way has been found to physically connect the Box to the other two systems without drastically impairing its performance. "It's the electronics. If they touch it, they change it," hissed Snake.

"Alone, the Box somehow intuits information from Creation and Brix and generates accurate futurisms, but they are random. It's not foresight unless someone is looking for it. Brix and Creation would foster focus if clear communication could be established."

Discussion ensued. The usual things at first but after a time, when they'd been talking about tunneling, Ramone admitted she had snuck down the trunk once or twice late at night after maintenance to visit the said systems. She found them affable she said. She even boasted of having all three in the same room. She justified her actions as homework. To better understand the needs of he she served, familiarity with his work was imperative. Snake was impressed, Pinn was not and ended the meeting.

On his way out, Snake applauded Pinn's extraordinary work where Ramone was concerned. "For a PA she's friendly, knowledgeable, and, judging by the excellent coffee she procured, was probably standing nearer to our desired outcome than anything else we have done lately. Relax, notwithstanding the untested intelligence, what could go wrong?"

Pinn took that as any deaf man would and went back inside to develop a firewall to keep Ramone out of Glenst Yng, but on second thoughts left a sovrapposizione nascosta, at the north wall that changed its coordinates regularly and irrationally.

*

A few days passed before Ramone said, "Stop. You can't ignore it," to a sulking Pinn.

Pinn didn't know what "it" was and did what he normally did in such circumstances; light a cigarette.

It has not been mentioned before how Ramone might appear, and sound. She looked and sounded not unlike her character in the game. Her hair was dark, she was slender, leggy, had a British accent, blue eyes, and really red lips. She also had access to a good range of weaponry. Pinn removed most of the weapons privileges and groomed her a little more like Fran Fine.

On this afternoon she was wearing a smart red frock with a thick, shiny black belt and similarly black cuissardes.

The short version of the conversation covered the following: Pinn's attempts to invent the future and how sitting on his few laurels was not getting it done.

How it was conveyed was thus. Ramone thanked Pinn for leaving a secretive access to the trunk before embarking on a fairly cryptic monologue. My grasp on the leaps proposed here are basic. So basically, if we don't focus on the why's, how's and implicities, it is all very simple. In Ramone's words, Pinn needed to put Creation, Brix, the Box and anything else he wanted to work with it into a single outcome acceptable to the parameters of what he was trying to type. After that, processing output into values is only a matter of statistics.

Pinn lit another cigarette.

"You know someone who can do that part for you," Ramone continued.

"What part," Pinn asked?

"Statistics. If you had a more orderly entity to work with now, the road forward might be clearer."

A long silence followed.

"Who do I know," Pinn asked finally?

"Grubb Gadjet, a stat mech savant who makes glyptic universes for the supernatural trail on the side. You went to school with him."

Ramone had already emailed Grubb as Pinn saying he was very interested in his work and would like to discuss a situation which he (she) outlined vaguely. When Grubb expressed an interest, Ramone booked his flight.

"I don't remember a Grubb," said Pinn. "With a name like that you would think I would."

"You will, he'll be here tomorrow."

They had never met. Both had attended the same school, Strathfield Polytech, but ten years apart.

"Oops," said Ramone.

The Grubb, as he came to be known, knew a little about Pinn's work. To him, Pinn was trying to marry a tactilian influence with a mechanical one in an AI environment. Grubb didn't know how the tactile bit worked but he had been treating it, in his math, as a disease that produced symptoms and found, to his surprise, there could be a very simple solution if the problem was what he thought it may be.

Pinn invited him to stay.

Snake and the Grubb got on swimmingly. Snake was happy to work with someone a little more forthcoming, and over a number of weeks the pair came up with the configuration of a basic structure they thought would work for the system they were trying to establish.

A meeting was held at Cubus and the model was presented.

The Grubb, whole name, Grubbastard Disaplegajet, described the position. "This is a halfway house," he said, holding up a device that looked like a small egg. "Everybody so far is present, and you can call them individually or all at the same time if you like, but the information they present remains untreated. It is not connected, so you get something that may or may not answer the question.

"As far as I understand it," he went on, "you want this machine to be convincing, to assure the user that what it is telling them will eventuate or at least be relevant. Nonetheless, bonding is the goal, and believability must be there from the outset. Ask it a question."

He handed Pinn the egg.

"How did you get the Box on board?"

"Not me, it."

"How did you get the Box on board," Pinn repeated?

Grubb huffed at his run being broken and flopped back in his chair.

Snake answered. "We let it do its thing in the device that the querier wears or holds. After a question has been asked, Creation and Brix collect the information it sends to the user at epidermis level, do their thing on it then send it back to the same place a couple of milliseconds later. The user gets the treated outcome. On the odd occasion the Box overrules the other two."

"Is that an issue?"

"Not so far, but we don't like it."

Pinn nodded through his thoughts but said nothing.

After a time, the Grubb leaned forward and said again, "ask it a question."

"The machine is not supposed to know of me," Pinn pointed out.

"One part of it doesn't," responded Grubb, "and that is very cool by the way, would love to know how you did that, but the other two do. For the sake of argument, ask a question. It will answer."

"To whom am I indebted for the Box?"

"Depends upon," said Creation.

"To which box," said Brix.

"You refer, said the Box.

"Cute," said Pinn.

"Exactly," said Grubb. "What we can harness so far is Creation emanating information backwards, Brix processing it forward, and the Box at indifference. Nice start, but it's missing the voice of God."

Ramone told Grubb she quite liked the voice of God jest as she hosted Snake and he out the door a short time later.

4.

Pinn was also taken by Grubb's "voice of God," remark and set about trying to imagine how he could create such a presence. He couldn't. Instead, he opted for a triposing threesome. The muses: the mother, the lover, and the layer out - hag. Minɛrva, Mia and Miss Trust.

There was no chieftainess.

Minɛrva, the mother was responsible for logic, art, wisdom and health. Her avatar was a dark haired, robed woman with gentle eyes and a golden sash. In certain lights, shadows had to be taken into consideration. She was not the doting mother but rather the complex. She spoke with control in an attractive timbre. She could be nurturing but focused on opportunity.

Mia, the lover. As things developed, it was learnt it was possible to heighten a person's experience, sight wise or otherwise, by feeding preferred information gleaned from that person, subliminally, at the same time as they viewed imagery, listened to music, read an article, etc. It involved a slightly slower, but unnoticeably so, process that became known as the Zembla Pass. It was surprisingly effective and could either enhance or taint a result. Whilst the Zembla Pass was used by all the muses at one point or another to emphasize various futurisms, it was only ever applied to the root level of one muse. Mia.

Industry, pleasure, ambition and treachery.

Mia's avatar represented the lover you wanted to see.

Responsible for duty, desire, daring and death, Miss Trust, the layer out, presents as the perfect PA. She knows more about you than you do about yourself and thinks you are an idiot. She wears a uniform style, grey, below the knee skirt suit, white blouse and regulation thick, black heels. She is slim but disturbingly breasty and wears large glasses. Her eyes are a leery flax behind them. She punishes her long grey hair, paints her lips darkly and begrudges the other two's complexion. She gets her jollies working with your futile attempt to arrest the inevitable.

*

As ReadMe approached release, the Grubb came up with a conundrum. People who don't have ReadMe might want to protect themselves against people who do. "Paranoia is free," he said, "and many people, especially rich ones, take it up."

After a time Pinn responded, "the only way to protect yourself against ReadMe is to get it."

"I know that, and you know that," continued the Grubb, "but by creating protection we could pick up an extra twenty percent of the total not in participation. It would fill in a lot of blank spaces we would not otherwise fill. Wildly useful. We need to come up with a product by an unrelated company that defends the user against those using ReadMe. If we don't do it, somebody else will."

Pinn: "Sell them a ReadMe Black?"

Grubb: "No, sell them a Watch My Back."

5.

After the meeting, all three walked out to the car park together. Grubb hurried off.

It was one of those sunny spring mornings spun more to please the eye than warm the flesh.

Pinn and Snake ambled. As they approached Snake's car, a dark SUV, Pinn said, "I am not comfortable working with a black ReadMe, especially if it it's called what he said."

"Leave it," said Snake. "We'll get to that. Meanwhile, here's a new one for you. Mia has been talking to me lately about you and Renée."

"Why? What did you ask her?"

"That's just it, I didn't ask her anything. She came out with it when I was more occupied with an uncooperative egg I was trying to poach. She said Ramone told her to tell me to tell you Renée would give you a son around the vernal equinox."

"Unlike Mia to cede to anyone."

"Yes, except it was to Ramone."

"I couldn't bring myself to restrain Ramone."

"I know."

"When is the next vernal equinox," asked Pinn?

"March, next year."

*

After Snake drove off Pinn wandered down to the house. There was nobody home. Michelle, Justine, Catherine and Izabella were out at a school thing, and Gustaf and Greta had gone to the movies.

Pinn vaguely knew that.

He got a sweet, white coffee from the kitchen and wandered down toward the glassed partition on the eastern side of the slightly steaming pool, just in time to see Renée launch herself from it in a single movement. She was wearing a bright yellow one piece bathing suit. She stood, tilted her head back slightly, shook her hair, then raised both elbows so she could slide her fingers through it. She was in profile and slow motion. She went for a light blue towel when she was done. Gene was guarding it. She dabbed her face once or twice then began to wrap the towel around herself sarong style. At that point she noticed Pinn standing there. Pinn didn't pretend he was not watching, and she didn't leave in haste.

Pinn was thinking about Ramone after he walked away. He stretched out on a deck chair. He was not happy she was manipulating the muses.

He slept.

"You grunt like a pig," she said, "I don't know how you can sleep through it, let alone anybody else."

Pinn awoke with an extra loud snaug.

"Come with me," she said turning and leaving without waiting.

Pinn mustered himself and started after her.

He was led down the arcade to the elevators to Cubus, where they rode one up.

The lifts were unusual. The roof and walls xylophoned away near the top so by the time you reached Cubus you were standing, unencumbered, in open space.

"Sit," said Ramone, who then strode off.

Pinn knew what she meant.

Pinn thought it would have been late in the morning and was surprised by how dark it was, and the stunning stars cape beyond the dome.

Ramone whistled. Pinn proceeded toward the lit bit of the room. There, on a comfortable looking padded onyx platform with gold angular trim about five feet high, the platform, not the trim, Gene reclined Sphinx like. Diamond Dog like really, he didn't haunch is hind legs. Ramone excused herself and went off to sit on a nearby, polished, diorite pill. She lit a cigarette. She was wearing sheik black chic with high, thin heels. A pale fire motif fluttered through her ensemble.

"You have no sons," stated Gene, drawing Pinn's attention.

"Men have daughters, Gentlemen have sons," said Pinn.

"I am not sure what that has to do with anything," said Gene, "but I am pretty sure it's the other way around."

"Whatever. Why would I need a son?"

"You are not bright are you Pinn," said the dog?

The dog didn't actually mouth the words he was speaking but his vocal system was involved. His voice was formed by a throaty, inflective cuing refined by tongue distancing and lip quivers. Or that's what it seemed like to Pinn.

"Renée will be the mother," Gene continued. "She is of acceptable lineage, has spectacular health and is bright to boot. The stories about blondes are wrong."

"You only think she's bright because she took you off that woman," said Pinn. "It probably argues the opposite."

Gene stood, performed a neat U turn on the narrow platform, then took the steps at the back to join Pinn on the floor below. A chair appeared for Pinn and both sat. They were at a comfortable distance apart and almost eye to eye. The dog was taller.

"You remind me of someone," said Pinn.

The dog contorted a little right and scratched behind his left ear with his hind paw rapidly for a few seconds before sitting upright again. You could see he enjoyed it. His tongue hung out and he had that look on his face.

"Why Renée? Why not Michelle or Catherine," asked Pinn?

"It has to do with entropy."

"Entropy, really?"

"Yes," said Gene. "You know a bit about chemical reactions. The more intense the event, the more widespread the influence. If we go with Catherine or Michelle, we may end up with second or third child syndrome situations. And again, time says now."

"Feels a bit like I," said Pinn.

"You have become soft Pinn," said Gene getting up to go, "especially with your women. We need an alpha male like Justine and Izabella are alpha females. And we need him now. Renée will give you a son with ambition. Atlaseze will be his name."

"You grunt like a warthog," said Catherine sweeping by brushing Pinn's feet with her things. "Here come the girls."

Both landed on Pinn's abdomen, individually, from oldest to youngest, winding him. They cackled gleefully at his gasps. Pinn tickled. There was squealing, squirming, more gasps and giggles. Everybody ended up on the floor. Izabella scuffed a knee. Pinn found his breath.

6.

After the family had been issued the first ReadMe appliances, Nellie made an unannounced but not unexpected visit to Cubus to see Pinn. The weather was yet to warm. Nell wore a full length ermine coat while otherwise dressed as if off to play tennis.

Her daughters were not overly interested in the new ReadMe appliances they had been given to test. They preferred their current devices. Nellie, however sensed value and sought edification from the creator.

By this time, Ramone could appear holographically anywhere in Cubus, not just on screens, and greeted Nellie at the door. Nellie walked through her. Pinn rose.

"Always a pleasure," he said as she neared.

Both smiled, went through the usual politeness's, touched cheeks, then settled on lounges opposite.

Pinn offered to take Nellie's coat, but she refused.

Leaning forward, she said, "tell me about this thing," pointing to the appliance on her wrist.

"It's ReadMe," said Pinn, "as you know. It's a tool to make your life easier."

"In what way?"

"Any way you want," responded Pinn. "Ignoring mundaneness's like the mechanics of calling, texting, creating a reminder, paying a vendor and monitoring your health, it can be a companion, an advisor and more."

"An advisor?"

"Yes. It, they, the muses can make extraordinarily accurate predictions about personal likelihoods up to a point. Used in moderation, it could save you time, anxiety, and energy."

"Really," said Nell leaning back looking more like a gangly legged teenager unaware of herself than the closed buck canyon of her otherwiseness.

Pinn got up and fetched coffee. She sat up.

After a sip or two she asked, "do you use it?"

The dog arrived via an elevator and trotted over. He sat next to Nellie, one paw on her left tennis shoe. She didn't seem to notice.

"Of course. I talk to the girls a lot; they are my children after all. But I am not a big believer in predicting futures. The ability to create the illusion of foresight was thrust upon me by some unknown source. All the way up predictions, by their very nature, are guesswork at best and only seem predictive, in our case, through the mischievousness of confronting the inquirer with their own statistics coherently."

"Does Miss Trust ever mention Snake to you?"

"No, But I don't ask."

"According to Snake you have developed ReadMe, up to a level twelve. At this point you have us all on a level four, except Snake and Grubb, where did you get him from, who are on a level six. I am assuming your level is unrestricted."

Pinn said nothing.

"At level four, the muses are very nice, and one even indicates an appropriate time for ablutions, but at level six, the world begins to change."

"How did you get to level six," Pinn wondered out loud?

"Snake works as much for me as he does for you," said Nell. "On level four if I ask any of the muses a simple question like, what will this year bring? What I get is; Minɛrva, the world will keep turning, Mia, prosperity is possible, and Miss Trust, the seeds will be sown.

"Digging a little deeper into what Miss Trust was referring, at level six, we find seeds not to be allegorical but rather, a highly likely future, infactedness.

"If you get a bit more specific and ask what will happen in, say, the forthcoming month. Minerva answers, it's not money that makes the world go around, Mia, yippy eye owe tie aye, and Miss Trust, here we go.

"It's tedious. You have to ask the right question."

"There is no right question," said Pinn, "there is a relationship to be built, preferred, but a good question is always a good question."

"Miss Trust talks about the influence of the Box in the final outcome, a fluke level."

"Miss Trust is resentful by nature," said Pinn. "The Box only works with presence. Being there. So, to it, no future can exist beyond anything the subject cannot consciously feel as an influence at the time of questioning. Creation and Brix illusionate a Box projection by adding their biscuits before it is interpreted by whichever muse was called upon for the information. The fluke level needs much to be invoked."

"It seems like you need to know the future to ask the right question," said Nellie dismissively, "that needs to be fixed. Let's talk."

"Do you want something Nellie," asked Pinn?

"Yes."

Both sat back crossing their legs in opposite directions. Nellie wrapped her coat over her knee.

"How can I help," said Pinn?

"The chatter amongst the girls, the muses, is that tippences are failing, and because the girls, Michelle and

Catherine are not following, fair warning cannot be relayed."

"So," said Pinn?

Nell found a cigarette and lit it herself. "These are my girls and I have a concern. And it was your application that fed it to me."

"No, it was you who pursued something with it. You want to know the future and truthfully, this technology proports to know it, but, as I said Nell, all you are getting is professional likelihoods. The future is a wish on a stick on one side and futile fear on the other. It's an insubstantial, a fantasy, limiting, or ted."

"Yet you read your horoscope daily."

"I do," said Pinn, standing and wandering off. "What do you need," he asked, taking a seat at a workstation a few paces away?

Nell joined him and sat on the corner of his desk, both feet on the floor.

"At least Michelle needs to be told," she said.

"Told what," asked Pinn? "And by who?"

"Whom."

"Whom."

"I would prefer for her to hear it from Miss Trust," said Nellie.

"Why can't you tell her yourself?"

"She wouldn't believe me. Well, she would, but it would be less confronting and easier to accept if it were to come cold and matter of fact from Miss Trust."

"Can't be done."

"Why not?"

"The muses are designed not to offer anything unless asked. It has to do with intrusion and other things that can potentially bully a diminishing capacity. They can only respond to requests. Michelle would have to ask Mia specifically about whatever it is to which you allude," said Pinn.

"My point, but not true," said Nel. "Snake told me Ramone got Mia to talk to him." She went back to the couch.

"You just walked through her on the way in," said Pinn, "not the act of someone seeking a favor."

"I thought you could help me."

Pinn returned to his couch and sat spread legged. "Maybe I can," he said, "what do I have to do?"

"Have Ramone tell Miss Trust to talk to Michelle."

"Anything else?"

"No, she will know why."

7.

On June 21, 2014, Renée, Michelle and Catherine conceived. In that order.

Catherine was away in Stockholm. She had been there a few times lately.

Pinn awoke at the usual time and went down to the pool to contemplate swimming a few laps. Sometimes he did. Sometimes he didn't. On this morning, he smoked a cigarette, then did.

For those who don't swim, swimming is a simple pleasure. It's usually done in a semi weightless, wet environment whose viscosity is nurturing. Most folks who do it willingly do it almost naked too, so the experience encompasses much. Movement, immersion, breath, touch and lots more. Pinn wore yellow board shorts with a thick red trim whose fabric was X rated when wet.

Pinn got into his lapping and was feeling virile when he finished and left the pool. He strode toward his towel, picked it up and held it, unfurled, to his diaphragm with both hands enjoying the depth of his breath. Renée emerged from the door to the gym. She was wearing a red two piece and white frilly slip-ons. With one hand on the door handle, she stood like a drum majorette mid step. A high knee. Seeing Pinn, she changed her mind about a swim and disappeared back behind the door.

Since the dream, Pinn had made a concerted effort to avoid Renée generally, and Gene specifically. But Renée was the nanny, which meant she, and the dog, were with the children most times he came across them, and so could not help but become involved in whatever situations he walked into unless he wanted to ignore the children's exuberances and otherances altogether. The girls were not yet six. Still adorable though Izabella was a bit tetchy.

Enchanted, Pinn started toward the gym, but caught himself and stopped.

In the kitchen, from her wheelchair, hidden by the ruckus, Michelle watched.

It was Saturday morning, pancakes for breakfast. Greta usually handled the children for a pancake breakfast because the girls liked to get involved in the cooking process about then. It gave Renée an undisturbed hour or so.

Pinn remained motionless. Michelle said she could see the wheels turning and knew he was about to pursue. He did. He walked to the gym door and opened it, looked in, threw his towel off to a nearby chair on the outside, and went in closing the door behind him.

Michelle could barely contain herself. She knew what was going to happen and she wanted to see it. She wanted firsthand proof. She let out a low, guttural groan which, fortunately, caught nobody's attention.

Michelle rolled out of the kitchen and took a left at the hall. Her pace held restraint. When she got to the alcove before the house entrance to the gym she stopped. She did not want to burst in and disturb them. She wanted to see. Her only option was a porthole window in the door eighteen inches higher than she could reach from her wheelchair.

She seethed in her seat, she thought, for ages. All sorts of things went through her head which she hadn't thought of in ages. Then, twinkledustdom, she found herself standing, easily seeing everything through the portal.

It looked choreographed to Michelle but worked excellently for her. She saw what she needed to see.

The nymph, leaning against a fluted column that was not normally there was staring at Pinn's unseen groin. She began to writhe and move and two circumferences of the column later had peeled off the two pieces she had been wearing. The slip-ons remained on. As Michelle was thinking she had no bust, Renée turned to face the column. She raised her arms. From behind she revealed a divine, tear dropped, ad vanum.

Pinn dropped his board shorts and started toward her. She heard him approach and rotated ninety degrees right flipping her nipples on the flutes of the column as she moved.

Pinn squared up and presented his membership to both girls. He walked to a position where he could address Renée.

Michelle almost fainted.

Using musical time signatures, don't ask me why, Michelle described what followed as beginning in 2/4 then changing to 4/4 for a while before evolving into an astonishing 9 bars of 7/4 with deep, ever growingly urgent thrusts on the last three beats of each bar, before exploding into three bars of life enlightening 21/12s' in single strokes which lifted Renee's feet off the ground. It finished on drawn out, 2/4s' as it began, as the couple dripped down the column. Michelle was exhausted.

She plonked herself back into her seat seconds before Gustaf passed by. He had been down in the garage.

"Are you ok," he asked, spotting Michelle in the alcove?

Michelle did not answer, she wiggled a bit and smiled, bowing her head slightly.

Gustaf pushed the kitchen button on her machine and followed her there. He noticed she was slumped a little awkwardly in her chair, and the correction she made to reposition herself as they approached the kitchen seemed to involve voluntary leg movement. He shrugged it off and went on his way.

A black track suited Pinn arrived in the kitchen and his daughters assembled his favorite pancake.

Renée was not far behind. Her track suit was pink with white stripes down the sides. She wore her hair pigtailed, had on some eye highlights and a happy pink lippy.

Greta made Renée crepes with sugar and lemon juice which she ate with avarice.

Michelle went to her suite.

*

When Michelle stood, one would have thought she would have been overjoyed and that her recovery would be celebrated. She was, and it was, privately. It was an unusually primal day and recognition could wait.

Michelle ensured all the windows and viewable areas in her suite were securely shaded, shuttered and locked, and then rose from her chair.

Everything lit up. The touch of her instep not touching the floor resonated briefly, high buttockly, then cerebellumly. There were tingles here and tangles there. Tip to toe sensation was screaming and while lower body muscular fitness was down some, Michelle believed, with determination, she could stay on her feet long enough. She would summon Pinn to her room that night.

Like all marriages, there was some arbitrariness in the relationship Pinn shared with his wives. They had the right to invite him to their rooms at their whim. Reciprocity was unavailable. This had slowed down somewhat over the last couple of years so Pinn was both surprised and suspicious when he was invited by Michelle to her room. Her language was ambiguous.

Michelle missed dinner. Greta offered her excuses.

Pinn allowed Justine and Izabella to eat in front of a big screen instead of at the table. He, Gustaf and Renée ate in silence behind, before Pinn left his food and went to join his daughters who had also put their plates aside.

Greta had cooked nobody's favorite, Zuppa di Tippa with a charred Brussel sprout, pumpkin and walnut risotto.

*

Pinn arrived on time as expected and through the bathroom door as expected. House specs were skipped in chapter one.

As he stepped through the threshold Michelle held up her hand to stop him. She was sitting in her wheelchair by a fluted column that was not normally there. Her hair was down. She wore a silk robe that revealed a cleavage he hadn't seen in some time. The room was lit provocatively, and sweet incense smoldered somewhere.

"Wet them and put them on," she said indicating his dry, yellow and red board shorts on a small table to his right.

Pinn returned to the bathroom with his board shorts, soaked them, wringed them and put them on.

Pinn thought two outcomes possible when he returned to the room. The first was Michelle had seen him with Renée earlier and would shoot him with a handy revolver the moment he emerged. The second an unlikely fantasy that included domination and subservience. It didn't matter to him which role he played.

As Pinn re-entered, Michelle stood. Again, you would think something would be made of this moment, but again, it was ignored.

She moved toward the column, dropped her robe and leaned her back against it. She was wearing nothing but a modest silver chain around her waist. She did not have the lower body strength to do a three-circumference writhing striptease. Pinn was enraptured. He remembered those... why he... the way.... But never...

She turned to face the column. Pinn, having already dropped his shorts, would have fallen to his knees then and there and walked to her on them had she wished it. But she didn't. She wanted what Renée got and rotated ninety degrees right. Her breasts swept and then embraced the column.

She didn't get it, she said coyly. She would not elaborate. Not even in musical time signatures.

*

Meanwhile in Stockholm on that night, Catherine went out with John John Jonny Johnson, or J. to his friends, for the third time in as many weeks. They ended up back in her hotel suite. They ate at Gino Botticelli's Carnivore Clam, where they ordered oysters with marrow and Gino's glib gremolata. They drank appropriately, not excessively, or near enough, but still ended up feeling compelled, on this occasion, to copulate. And did.

Catherine had known John John for some time. He was always wandering in and out of her dealings. He was the sole heir to the Crimpla fortune, a wash concern that dealt in fine art and electronic theft among other things. It was likely John John was worth more than Pinn Pinn at the time.

John John had motivation beyond an overnight lust for Catherine. Catherine was aware of this but was not particularly concerned. John John expected Pinn already knew how to bend the spoon where questioned possibilities could be postulated into results with a good expectation of fruition in real time, and wanted access to the machine that could do it. Sleeping with Pinn's wife was possibly not the best strategy, but he considered he could win Catherine over and she would help him.

To her sister, Catherine described a clinical encounter that began in the bathroom with lots of cold surfaces and mirrors, progressed to the bedroom where she was tied to the bedstead and had her breasts signed then lashed with a peacock quill. It ended with John John being annoyingly insecure. He was quick too, Catherine noted. On both occasions. But not when it came time to leave.

8.

As it became clear all three girls were pregnant, there was disturbance in the house of Blingcrowd. "There will only be one legitimate child among the three," noted Nellie, who was not as liberal when it came to these things as one might expect.

Gorm loathed the involvement of the Jonny Johnson's. He never liked John, John John's father, ever since he rescued Nell late one afternoon by offering her a ride in his Gulfstream when she became stranded in London. They spent the night in Geneva at Le Richemond in the Royal

Armleder Suite, converted to include a separate bedroom, Nell assured Gorm. The following morning, after breakfasting at Le Jardin, John personally drove her the eighty kilometers to the estate in his racing red Maserati Grand Turismo.

Pinn was not happy either. His wife's infidelity could not go unnoticed though he knew it was a battleground on which he could not win. Catherine shot down his pitiful self-righteous indignation. She said it was a mishap, much like his own with Renée, and assured him it was unlikely to reoccur as she headed out the door on her way back to Stockholm.

Pinn's first son Sumonus was born on March 23, 2015, to Michelle. The following day Renee delivered his second, Atlaseze, in the morning, and Catherine delivered a girl, Lilita, in the evening.

*

Seven days later, ReadMe launched. In Europe first, then America a few weeks later. By early September, Pinn had appeared on the cover of several gossip magazines on both continents. Some reports used adulatory accolades to describe the product while others said it, ReadMe, was the herald of the devil himself. The breakdown of consensus was about sixty six, thirty four in your preference.

One of the stories presented by the accoladers showed a well to do chicken farmer, Jess Harper, from Berlin, Connecticut, who saw his fortune rise sharply after subscribing to a low level ReadMe package. A single page article with a picture of him and Mirabelle in a weekend magazine said Jess had been perturbed by incoherent utterances made by his demented and dying wife a few weeks before she passed. It had been playing on his mind the night he came across the spiel being put out by Global Daze on social media about its new product, ReadMe.

Amongst the blurb was the claim, the muses know all pasts and offer likely futures. Packages purchasable in bytes.

Jess said he didn't know what that meant but, on a hunch, bought himself a twelve-month, entry level subscription.

The morning after his device arrived, as he was about to go off and sit with Mirabelle, a more petite and lighter colored Lohmann Brown, his favorite chook (chicken) and companion since his wife died, even before his wife died, he remembered the "all pasts" part from the ReadMe blurb and decided to try it out. He read the manual that came with the appliance, then put it on and addressed Minεrva. He asked what it was his wife was trying to tell him in the days before her death.

The article said Minεrva said she, his wife, was trying to tell him about money she had stashed away over time, and where he could stick it. A lot of money. $24.3 million, which Minεrva then went on to help Jess recover.

The other side, the heralders of the rise of chaos were, as to be expected, grubby and dark. They inferred all sorts of crime and deviousness could be facilitated through the use of the system.

"It's all bupkis," said Snake. "You don't need ReadMe to embezzle, smuggle, abduct and murder. It's standard behavior for certain types. They have their quotas to meet like everybody else. But if you did use the muses to help, there would be an undeniable record easily accessible to anybody with a higher level of access to ReadMe, including law enforcement."

The Grubb concurred with Snake; "It's bupkis. But we do have a little glitch."

"Oh?"

"Yes. It happens on our level, level six."

"Go on."

"Level six has all the muses at the same capacity, thirty three point three percent. There is an equilibrium thing going on here that is hard to escape. No matter what prediction the muses make, either individually or as a group, they operate as if the prediction is right at a fifty one percent possibility or above.

"The muses, think they are right in the first place based on the principle that if you have fifty percent of something then it implies there is another fifty percent. But in our world, it is a lapse in awareness. The existence of the other fifty percent, in the context of that being questioned is a classical perspective, but in our world, things move on a gloxonomy scale and percentages are an assumption at best. No matter how well defined the circumstances are in a situation, the only value that holds any relevance is the one in hand. Everything else changes every instant. So, in effect, there is no such thing in the world of ReadMe as a defining percentage ratio."

"Your point," asked Pinn?

Snake took over. "If we were to drop percentage as an instruction to the muses and a description to the consumers and focus on time instead, we would be, realistically, more on point.

"The muses agree that if we were to make the changes we propose, business would increase significantly."

"You just said responses by the muses on level six, your level, are not accurate."

"I told you he would say that," said Grubb.

"They are accurate enough," continued Snake, "but they could be better. Our point. Modeling shows with the percentage calculation turned off, and that was hard to do, you had it shoved right down in there at the beginning, line eighteen I think, where it was obscured by symbols I've never seen before. Why would you do that? Rhetorical."

Snake raised his right shoosh finger and waggled it.

"We could not just delete the line for reasons only you would know so we inserted the words "dingle berries", in the middle of it, which seemed to work. The only side effect being the muses no longer have "percent" in their vocabulary. They can still calculate it due to their omniscient nature, but they no longer say the word.

"We found once that was bypassed and we gave the muses orientation from three perspectives: time, which was deemed finite; occurrence, which was deemed definite; and depth, which was deemed fiat, without calculating a percentage so early, the muses used more of the resources available to them and found uninhibited chance. The results were often way under or way over what the percentage might have been but that was because they were not confined to a closing argument from the outset. Things like the mental deflation of a mosquito splashing down in your wet nail polish, or what ghost you killed on the off ramp could be taken into account wholistically rather than individualistically, adding depth to the users' satisfaction levels."

"By what percent," Pinn asked?

"Twenty seven dingle berries," interrupted Ramone chuckling.

Snake and Grubb found that humorous too.

A large moth began to flap around and crash into the lamp that lit the table. It did so for a time before landing heavily at its base. It was a cossus cossus, a goat moth. Since everybody's attention was broken by the arrival of the lepidopterous insect who had just dropped by to die, Pinn suggested a short break.

"Why wasn't this picked up earlier," Pinn asked when everybody returned to the table?

Snake again: "We were busy. This whole thing came up in pretty near eighteen months. We didn't have the time or the personnel to do any definitive testing and you assured us all was good with the muses. A bit snake oilish on your part we thought. You sell predictions but you never look at them yourself in the context of your life or anybody else's."

"I know my future," said Pinn.

"Really."

"Yes. The is, is it."

Nobody commented.

"Will the changes you are proposing require any down time," asked Pinn?

"None," said Snake, "but it would happen more seamlessly if you were to assist. All we did for the current release was work out packages and user interfaces. But now, since we are performing surgery on the programming itself, which is complex, the potential to add to our problems increases significantly without a consultant with firsthand knowledge of the creatures' DNA."

Pinn pondered the off handed request for a few minutes, then addressed Ramone. They spoke together briefly before Pinn turned back to Snake.

"You cannot solve a problem from the same level on which it exists," he said. "I read that somewhere recently. To that end, you will both be elevated to a newly created developer level in ReadMe. There is wilderness there so you will have some work to do. Ramone will assist you with any technicalities. She will be available only in your offices at Glenst Yng and of course, here, though that's an imponderable – she gets more omnipotent by the day. You may not find Ramone's involvement to your liking. She is more demanding than I because she considers the muses to be her babies. They are not, they are mine, just as she is mine. Should any conflict arise between yourselves and Ramone, I will be available for consultation."

"Could a HAL situation arise," asked the Grubb?

"No. Ramone and the muses have no desire to save us from ourselves or anything else. They are observers and predictionaries. If we die, they…., whatever. But they, better than anybody, know perpetuity is an impossibility. We flatter ourselves with infinities."

The Grubb scratched his head and hawed like half a donkey. "You say," he said, "the insights that you, we, have developed into ReadMe were given to you. Forgive me, but couldn't that presuppose perpetuance?"

"No. The time frame is different, not indefinite. Let's just stick to what we think we know."

There was no conflict between Ramone and the boys, or little. Pinn had to discuss one thing; whether a muse could reveal an impending catastrophe, or dark event they could see lying in the questioner's future, when they were not specifically asked about it.

"No," said Pinn. "Muses may only respond to what they have been asked, and nothing else. If they see something dire about to unfold in the querier's life, example - Darren asks if Deidre will say yes when he proposes on Saturday and will she like the ring? The answer can be yes or no with whatever qualifications the muses care to add, but they may not tell Darren, Deidre is going to die six months later, three months pregnant, crossing the road, when a sink hole suddenly opens up and swallows her whole after a few days of particularly heavy rain."

9.

For the next couple of years things went swimmingly. Confidence was high, fortunes were favored, and opulence prevailed. There were ups and downs of course but in all, everything stayed on an even keel until Gorm suddenly died on April 1, 2017.

According to the coroner, he inhaled two passing bumble bees at the beginning of an almighty sneeze, something to which Gorm was prone, then couldn't expel them at the choo phase of the two-part reflex, and suffocated. Gustaf found Gorm tangled amongst the morning glory, *ipomoea indica*, on the sunny side of the house, presenting as almost the same shade of blue. Both hands were at his swollen throat. The paramedics, after a prolonged telephone call with someone at the hospital, pronounced him dead at the scene at 11:59 am.

Gorm's passing created a great wave in the sphere of what was once deemed his, and it took its toll emotionally and strategically on everyone within the family and quite a few beyond. A magnificent and appropriate funeral was staged at which Gorm was honorably received.

Nellie was inconsolable and wanted to know why there was no warning from ReadMe. Grubb had no problem throwing Pinn under the bus for the omission of that option. He even parodied Pinn's Deidre tale.

Nellie questioned Pinn's judgment, again, about hiring Grubb.

Snake excused himself and took the Grubb with him.

Below is a transcript of the discussion that ensued between Nell and Pinn.

Nellie: Did you know this was going to happen?

Pinn: No.

Nellie: Could you have?

Pinn: It is possible. Had I looked, I might have seen it.

Nellie: There is no facility in the system to warn of an impending disaster?

Pinn: No.

Nellie: Why? It seems to me to be a reasonable expectation. Even a good selling point for an appliance that purports to know the future.

Pinn: The future is tricky.

Nellie: When I asked Minεrva at breakfast if I could expect Gorm to be home for dinner and she answered, he could be late, I didn't think she meant, that, late. Did she know?

Pinn: I don't know.

Nellie: But the muses are forbidden to warn of anything if not asked specifically if I am to believe the Grubb.

Pinn: Yes.

Nellie: Why?

Pinn: While we suggest we know the future and can perform a few mind tricks to promote it, all we are really doing, as you know, is providing statistical probabilities. Good statistical probabilities thanks to the Grubb, which we already know are in the punters' preferred range. For better or for worse the punter nearly always ends up where he or she expects. It looks like fortune telling but it's not. We endeavor to enable confidence. We lead the horse to water. To go further would mean we actually did make predictions which is a highly suable area to breach.

Nellie: So, what you are saying then Pinn, is you don't believe in the gift, as you so often refer to it, you have been given.

Pinn: The logs show the incident was only a vague possibility in Gorm's case. A number of things had to happen for it to unfold as it did.

Nellie: Yet they did. Was anything else likely to unfold?

Pinn: No, not on the extreme side.

Nellie: I ask again. Do you believe in the gift you have been given and have been working to develop, or do you not?

Pinn: You put me on the spot here Nell, it's complicated.

Nellie: It's a yes or no question Pinn.

Pinn: Yes.

Nellie: Then it's time to put your big boys' pants on and find a way to include the real value of the product you are hawking.

10.

Pinched by his conversation with Nellie, Pinn spent a few weeks of long days and nights at Cubus. He was surprised one night when he shuffled into the house around 3:am to come across Izabella, Renée, and Michelle huddled at the lowly lit kitchen table. Catherine was in Paris.

Paranoid Pinn asked, "what's up?"

"Izabella had a nightmare," said Renée. "She is calm now. We shall be back in bed shortly."

Pinn made himself tea and took a seat at the table. Izabella was sitting directly opposite. She had her arms folded in front of her on the table with her forehead resting on them. He asked her to tell him about her dream.

Both mothers protested.

"We have just calmed her," said Michelle.

"It's late, we need to get back to bed," said Renée.

Izabella raised her head, then rested her chin on the backs of her hands, which she had also raised.

"It's your fault daddy," she said.

"Of course," said Pinn taking a sip from his cup. "Do tell."

Izabella squinted a semi-profile glare. Both exhausted mothers flopped back in their seats. Justine, who had been off to check on the younger children, joined the table to her father's left.

Izabella's dream sounded indeed like a dream. There was drama, there was perplexion, and things tended toward sinister.

She seemed to have a thing for birds. She talked about a pelican post, a pair of storm birds, and what she called a kitten bird, *catulus avem*, because it sounded like one.

The four of them, Izabella, the two birds, and the kitten had to get to the Pelican Post or something dreadful would happen. The dreadfulness was not revealed, only felt, and felt direr the closer they got to the pelican post.

Izabella could not remember the whole journey, but she did remember this: a short distance from the pelican's pole, as she turned onto the street where it was erected, the universe suddenly went haywire. A huge storm arose, things around began to collapse, and a wave grew up in the bay. The wave kept gaining height until it was a great wall. At first, it seemed like it was being held up by the storm winds but then, suddenly, everything stopped, the world stood still, including the gigantic wall of water. A great silence followed that seemed to go on forever. Then, as if somebody just remembered something, everything went back to normal and Izabella woke before the wall of water crashed down upon her.

"How old are you,' asked Pinn inflecting upwards a little, "sixteen? You sound like a born-again Christian."

"I am nine," replied Izabella with indignance, "and I don't know what a born-again Christian is."

She frowned, couldn't decide whether to cross her arms, or put her hands on her hips, so she did both, one after the other.

"Impressive recollection and erudition," said Pinn, "but how is that my fault?"

Izabella got off her chair and stepped tightly and with purpose around the table toward her farther in that way of hers. She waited while Pinn slid his chair away from the table with his heels so she could sit on his lap. She sat, quite upright, facing Justine.

"It was so real," she said leaning into her father, "and I know what I saw will happen in my lifetime."

"The world standing still, half a parting of the seas," said Pinn putting his arms around her. "It seems unlikely sweetheart. Dreams can seem so real."

With her voice fading, she snuggled in a little and said, "I know you know daddy."

When she dropped off to sleep, Michelle carried her back to her room. Renée and Justine left at the same time.

Pinn lit a cigarette, made himself another cup of tea and wandered outside to sit at a table by the pool. It was a still, dark, night. Not cold but not warm. A waxing moon hung over the lake. Pinn looked for shooting stars for a while but saw none. He considered that unlucky.

"Mind if I join you," he heard from behind?

"Not at all," Pinn responded, pleased it was Michelle and not Renée.

Michelle took a seat opposite and inadvertently brushed his knee with hers as she sat.

"What did she mean when she said, I know you know," asked Michelle?

"I don't know."

Michelle briefly leaned forward and put her elbows on the table but changed her mind and sat back. She was wearing a mother's robe that she let hang loosely in the low light.

"Really?"

"Yes."

"You have been gone a lot lately. What have you been doing?"

"I thought withholding or blocking what happens beyond that questioned was correct because the questioner, simply, without notice, is not equipped to cope."

"Sounds weak, but okay. Why are you doubting it now?"

"I'm not. That holds true. But it seems to me, we, the species, seem desperately willing to believe anything we are told, regardless of how incredulous, if presented predictionarily. So long as it is formulated and modulated as such, folks will happily cut off a digit or poke out an eye on the word of a soothsayer. I am not sure if that's a good thing or a bad thing."

"Sip your tea, Pinn, you need sustenance."

Pinn lit a cigarette.

"Over the last two weeks," he continued, "I have been questioning the muses about my involvement in future events."

"Unlike you my love," said Michelle.

"Notwithstanding the odd twink here and there, the expected was projected, but by the end of 2021, or a bit earlier, there is a change. Something is introduced."

"What?"

"I don't know. It feels, seems, like I am being steered. System diagnostics show no interference. If I keep pushing my future, October 11, 2024, does not exist for me. The day before does, as does the day after and ensuing days, but something happens on that day. I can't find out what, exactly. Everything seems to be normal but not. Interestingly, as I moved onward, early in 2025, Izabella, then age seventeen, has the same dream she had tonight, only with a little more detail. The scene in the kitchen earlier was pretty much as it will be then, except Catherine will be in Casablanca, Justine sits on Izabella's left and the three young ones, ten by then, will be present."

"Then she was right," said Michelle, laughing as if slapping a raised knee. "You did know, and you are to blame."

"No, I am not to blame," said Pinn. "It's unlikely I am the pivotal character in all this, but I did hedge my bet on the awareness part."

"Hedge is not the word. What now?"

"I like it when you get this way," said Pinn. "Would you mind leaning forward, putting your elbows on the table, and cupping your chin again."

"I am tired," said Michelle, doing it.

All went quiet. Quiet enough for each to hear the other's breathing. Then typically, Pinn got back to business. "If I reverse my position," he said, "about allowable responses when a muse sees a dramatic event occurring beyond which the user queried, we will still not be, in any absoluteness, predicting anything. But since it is the next step up, it will be believed that that is exactly what we are doing."

"You over think things," said Michelle sitting upright with a bounce and an I'm off to bed smile. "Talk to Snake.

Wasn't he the time mechanic with a deft apunkathese way back when?"

She stood, stretched, leant forward and pecked Pinn's forehead. "Get to bed," she said.

11.

Not since Sai Chakrabarti in 1907 had anybody demonstrated the Indian rope trick in public and gotten away with it until, in 1994, at the age of fifteen, Snake, then Bosely Bumstead, sorted out a bullying problem by performing it.

The legend goes; after he'd turned the other cheek to Scoby Scutts, with no cheek left to turn, Bosely convinced Scoby, he could make him disappear in front of all his friends if he did not beat him up again.

There was shoving, disbelief, and derision from the group before Scoby said, "go on then."

Bosely was on his way home from recorder class. Unlike Sai, who performed the trick in the town square of a small village just outside Bangalore in front of an enthusiastic tourist with a brand new movie camera, Snake did it on a hand ball court behind the toilet block with a riled audience of five.

He took his backpack off, took his recorder from it then dropped the backpack at his feet. It landed neatly.

Turning to Scoby, Bosely said: "In a moment I am going to sit down and begin to play my pipe. A rope will rise from my backpack and will continue to rise. When I nod, you are to climb the rope. Don't worry, it will carry your weight and be easy to climb. Keep climbing until you disappear."

A silence fell among the group. Some had bewildered half grins on their faces. Birds chirped and raucous youngsters played off in the distance.

"Everyone except Scoby, take six steps back," Bosely ordered. "Scoby, you take three."

Nobody moved until Scoby did.

Bosely sat cross legged on the ground and began playing his recorder like a snake charmer. He had to bumble bee into the pipe to get the instrument to sound that way. Shortly, a sturdy rope emerged from Bosely's backpack. Everybody took a step back, including Scoby. The rope rose and after a time Bosely nodded. Scoby was reluctant to proceed and remained that way despite being egged on and nudged forward by the more brazen members of his cohort.

Bosely stood. Still playing his monotonic exotica, he began to dance in a circle, twisting and twirling around the rope and a confused and embarrassed Scoby. He picked up pace. Finally, Scoby put his hand on the rope.

Once on the rope, Scoby's enthusiasm grew. He and the rope disappeared when he was about fifteen feet up in the air in what seemed like a very short time.

Snake stopped playing his pipe, dropped it into his backpack, picked up his belongings, and began to leave.

He was roughly stopped. The cohort wanted Scoby's return. Immediately. Snake said Scoby will return in due course unless he, Bosely, is harmed. In which case, he may never return. Nobody was happy. Snake advised everybody to go home. Everything will be all right, he said.

The following day when Scoby's parents noticed Scoby hadn't been home, and after they had talked to some of his friends, they went to the police. Bosely was hauled in and questioned. He told the police he had not seen Scoby the previous afternoon. He had gone straight home after recorder class to babysit his younger sister so his mother could go to work.

Bosely's story checked out. Times were confirmed by his mother, her boss, and Miss Sharpe, the recorder teacher. He couldn't have been where they said he had been. Officers were reluctant to tell the story of how he allegedly played his recorder to entice a rope to advance skyward from his backpack, which Scoby then climbed up and into disappearance.

They took him home.

Two days later, Scoby was found by Jacinta Corby in the girl's toilet block in front of the handball court during the morning recess break smelling of tequila and waving a hefty lit cheroot about. He could not recall how he got there, why he was wearing a pink, mink jock and pec armor, or where he had been for the last sixty-six hours.

With perseverance, the above story can be verified.

It is mentioned here because when Pinn asked Snake about it many years back, Snake dismissed it as a bit of playful time whispering. He had just read about the Indian rope trick that morning.

A couple of years after the Scoby incident, Snake tried to demonstrate time whispering at a meta-science symposium for under eighteens in Brussels. It was reported in the Böcstardt Gazette a week later that his presentation was clever, but the use of hypnotics and other trickery could not be ruled out. Snake gave up after that and turned his attention to other things.

Pinn was afraid of going the full Monty with ReadMe. He worried about the neuroses it would cause the obsessed. He worried it would speed up time since more people would be looking into it more often. But most of all he worried about himself being dacked. Getting his trousers pulled down publicly for allowing his machine to posit outcomes which, depending on how they turned out, could be construed as misleading, or misconstrued as leading. He had become accustomed to his life of privilege.

Pinn took Michelle's advice and late the following afternoon had Gustaf drive him down to Glenst Yng to catch up with Snake in his office. Snake was surprised but not unpleasantly so by Pinn's unannounced visit.

It was approaching the cocktail hour so Snake offered Pinn his usual drink, a Boiler maker. As Snake was preparing the drinks, Pinn took four modest reefers from a compartment in his sardonyx cigarette case. "Noosa Heads," he said, handing one to Snake.

Both skolled their bourbon and smoked quietly through their first beer.

It was not until Snake began pouring the second round did Pinn address the issue that brought him there.

"Beelzebub will have dibs on our product if we take it to the level consensus says we should."

"I didn't think you believed in the devil," said Snake, "but since you have doubts, he already has."

"I know there is evil."

"Evil is just live spelt backwards as God is dog. We know it takes all kinds. Everything we see in the world we are creating proves it. In fact, evil, as it is understood, is probably more prevalent than good if you were to consider it in the degrees it's applied."

"You are not making me feel any better."

"Not my job," said Snake. "There is something you want, and you need my help. What is it? It's unlike you to be coy Pinn."

"I want complete immunity from every country in the world for anything that would ever be said, implied, or omitted by ReadMe's muses under any circumstances."

Snake offered a wry grin but no response.

Pinn calmed.

"Can we softwarically build in protection against the law from the people whose desires or dreams don't come true after one of the muses implies it is possible?

"Prediction fruition or non-fruition," Pinn continued, "is an emotional time for folks who indulge in that sort of thing. The upside is burgeoning belief and some loyalty. The downside is getting sued and death threats, especially if a loser had anybody else play a part in their decision making. Their defense is always coercion, which is very difficult to disprove using the cold transcripts from the machine."

"Include a disclaimer like any other bookie."

"We will."

"A good disclaimer, keep transcripts out."

"We will try, but it's complicated. I would feel more comfortable with something more assuring like fudge. Can we not fudge something in the mechanical timing which would legally excuse us should we be taken to court?"

"Like what?"

"An intervening mist. A softwarical Indian rope trick."

'A softwarical Indian rope trick," repeated Snake.

"Yes. Have whatever information ReadMe has collected on any situation destined for court whispered out of existence as whimsically as the subject in the trick at presentation."

"That's the fudge?"

"Yes."

"No."

They were sitting on couches around a largish coffee table. Pinn leaned back and put his feet upon it.

Snake got up and wandered over to the bar to fix another round.

As he bustled about, he spoke.

"I can only question my future as that is all the system permits. But its responses do consider relationships both intimate and plutonic in the questions the user asks. From what I can tell, again from my perspective, nothing overly dramatic or disastrous is going to happen to you in the near future."

"I have seen that myself," said Pinn. "Thank you."

"Does your access allow you to see a world future," asked Snake? He put Pinn's bourbon and beer close to his feet."

"Yes, if I were to look."

"Wouldn't a worldview help you?"

"No. Has Miss Trust talked to you about fate and destiny?"

"Yes, she says a pencil's fate is graphite and wood shavings. A comet's destiny can be worldly."

"To me she says fate is being taught how to grow wheat. There is no destiny from there."

"Quite the propagandist," said Snake. "Getting back to where we were. In my future life, according to the muses, all things move along more or less smoothly until October 2024 when something happens. I don't know what. Each muse uses a trance like vagueness to describe it and their stories only match in abstract. Whatever happens, however, doesn't happen to me. It happens to you, but it affects us all. It's not your death or any other dire outcome you may think of because by May the following year, you are bridled in gold."

"Bridled in gold?"

"Yes, favored, captured, Minɛrva wasn't clear."

Pinn told Snake about his experimental forays into the future and how all is good for him until November 2021 when some sort of interference turns up in his life. It is not generated from a breach of the system but rather from a hitherto unknown scient equation in Creation that wrote itself into existence and then executed itself.

"It feels like I am being groomed," said Pinn.

"It sounds like you are stoned," said Snake. "Go home. It's late, the sun is almost up."

12.

A year later, ReadMe's futuristic prediction add-on was going well. It didn't create anywhere near the problems Pinn imagined it might, thanks largely to Dip Fletcher, the newest arrival, who packaged the ReadMe extension expensively and sold it in single units. Dip was another one of Ramone's discoveries. He was a spin doctor and legal guy.

According to Ramone, he was the one who defended Yimmy in that espionage case and got him off by proving he did it. He also proved six was nine when ………

Pinn stopped her. "Ok," he said, "get him here and we'll chat."

"His car is pulling up outside," she said.

As with the Grubb, Ramone wrote to Dip, but this time as Pinn's assistant. She said Pinn admired his work immensely and then went on to tell him of Pinn's concerns when it came to the owner of a machine that predicts a future that doesn't come true, ending up in court in civil action.

His response was; one would assume the owner of a machine that could predict the future would foresee such outcomes approaching and do something about them before they became an issue. Having said that, Miss Trust says, so should I. I would be happy to come along and look into Pinn's concerns for my usual fee.

Ramone booked his flight.

After a brief chat, Pinn upgraded Dip's ReadMe status significantly and thanked him for agreeing to investigate the situation. He fitted in well with the Snake and the Grubb and stayed.

*

Two years later a pandemic came along. On December 31, 2019, the World Health Organization was informed of cases of pneumonia of unknown origin. A novel covid virus was identified by authorities as the cause on January 7, 2020 and was temporarily named 2019-nCov. It turned out to be quite the Ney Years Eve gift.

A lot of ReadMe users saw the result of the coming pandemic early. Sickness, restrictions, and worse. They began buying up every food stuff and cleanliness item they could, filling closets, cellars, attics, newly bought freezers, and any other storage facility they could fill. It was not the actual cause of the supply chain collapse, which arose a few months later when all sorts of population movement became restricted from local to global, but a good percentage of ReadMe users, a little over nine hundred million, did start the ball rolling.

"It would be good advertising," said Dip, "if we could soften, or lose the glaring self-interest aspect."

Catherine had to quarantine in a hotel for fourteen days after returning from Hong Kong. Unable to travel to her places of work, she set up offices in the arcade on the way to Cubus and installed Brittany and Smitten, her right and left-hand man, respectively, in separate apartments in the guest's quarters.

When lock downs came, due to the rampant spread of the virus, Michelle, Renee, Greta, and sometimes Nellie, home schooled the children. Nellie bought an electric all weather buggy to commute from the main house to the garden house.

Pinn rarely left the estate. Visitors to Cubus, though never many, dwindled a little.

Snake and Stheno, a gorgon, Global Daze's cyber security specialist, took up residence at Glenst Yng. A small team of maintenance guys stayed on as well turning the staff facilities into a gamers' paradise. All other employees got back to work online from home in due course.

By the middle of the year, Pinn wanted to shut ReadMe down, except where medical contracts existed, due to the extraordinary amount of hardship it was projecting.

"You have to take the good with the bad," said Snake.

"Whose, theirs or ours," asked Pinn? "The bulk of our subscribers can only see a month or two ahead. It feels like we are monetizing anguish."

"It's the bleep on the radar at the moment," said Grubb. It's always there in one sector or another. This one has not, as yet, approached an influence the operators' manual calls worrying. We will adapt, protect ourselves with vaccines and move on."

13.

Late one Thursday evening in September 2021, after a sublime meatball pasta, which he nuked and ate alone, Pinn wandered down to the lounge to recline in his favorite chair. He settled back and began to marvel at his wonderous existence. The magnificent, snow-dressed mountains across the way being mauled by a brutal full moon, the diamond at the foot of the lake, his good fortune, his family who were all in bed, his comfort.

He was joined by the dog. He did not make much of an effort to pet him but soon began talking to the animal as if it could respond.

"Starting tomorrow," he said, unreclining and sitting upright, "I am going to shun my cyber existence for a few hours and take myself down to town and walk myself along the quay. In fact, I will do it every Friday from now on, masked if necessary, and attempt to find that which is lacking in my life. I feel there is something."

Gene's ears went forward. It looked like he frowned. He trotted off.

"Adventure," said Ramone who appeared sitting on a chair to his right. "That's what you are lacking. Would you like to know what happens on your ninth stroll?"

"No, thank you," said Pinn. He removed his ring. Turned Ramone off.

*

As the ReadMe hardware evolved, it became clear the user did not necessarily need to carry or wear an appliance. It could be implanted as a chip, then facilitated by peripherals like jewelry, eyewear, clothing, and even tattoos. The implant procedure was cheap. It could be done by any experienced body piercer, but the chip and peripherals were not. Despite that, due to its ability to become exclusively tailored, and an abundance of wealth in first world countries, the preference grew in popularity.

The implant, however, was not for Pinn. Pinn had an unreasonable belief which he attributed to his early, undisciplined, reading, that once you deliberately cut into the human body you let in an air, which led to contamination and death.

Pinn's ReadMe was administered by nine rings, all except one, silver or white gold. Some rings were studded with gems. Two with diamonds, one with a single pale emerald. Each had its function. He wore three rings on each of his pinkies, two on his left ring finger and one on his right.

The singular ring on Pinn's right ring finger, void black if there is such a color, made of titanium sup, was as close as Pinn had to an off button without physically removing all his rings. It was more like a "do not disturb" flag. To activate it, Pinn had to touch the ring with the thumb of the same hand. When he did that, to the casual observer the ring looked as if it had been removed. It hadn't, but that's another explanation. To those who knew Pinn, it was notice he was offline.

Only Ramone could override the state, and only if an approaching situation was deemed threatening according to rules Pinn and she had agreed upon.

*

The following morning Pinn rose around 6 am, took a quick shower, put on jeans, a white houndstooth flannelette shirt which he did up to the neck, a calf leather jacket, and boots. He buzzed Gustaf who brought the car up from the garage. The Bentley. Pinn said he was hoping for something a little more jaunty. A few minutes later Gustaf had swapped the Bentley for the Stinger. As Gustaf held the door open for Pinn to enter, Gene suddenly appeared from nowhere and darted between Gustaf and Pinn to take a seat on the front passenger seat of the car.

"He obviously can't drive," said Gustaf, making an attempt at levity.

"Get him out," said Pinn, not feeling it.

Neither Gustaf nor Pinn could budge the animal who was not afraid of baring his teeth, producing froth, and behaving aggressively if physically approached.

They gave up trying to remove him after Gustaf sustained a small fang scrape on his left wrist, which bled for longer than both expected.

Pinn called Renée. He and Gustaf were standing beside the open front passenger side door of the Stinger looking at an unbuckled dog, sitting upright, staring straight ahead, ready to go.

Gustaf could hear Renée laughing as Pinn explained the situation to her.

He was less huffy than he had been earlier and walked away to chat with Renée. He apologized for waking her. His body language said things were going well. Shortly he returned to the car, flicked a switch, and with a few giggled words from his mistress, the dog fumbled out of the vehicle and trotted off.

Pinn was about to close the door of the car when he noticed Gustaf nursing his wrist.

"Would you like me to drop you at the hospital," he asked?

*

Pinn enjoyed the drive down the mountain. He enjoyed his walk along the promenade and patted himself on the back for his efforts during the casual drive home. As for actual detail, there was none. He didn't know where he parked, couldn't tell you if he had walked past or talked to anybody during his stroll, if the sun was out, if there was water in the lake, how the car knew the way. Time just went by.

The following week, he had more presence. There was mild vexation and incidents as detail began to register about the world outside. By week five, Pinn was taking the dog with him.

On week nine, November 12, 2021, an unusually cold and windy morning, Pinn's stroll unfolded thusly: The dog, in laced, waterproof Ugg boots and a stylish oil skin coat (Renée was sometimes particular about how Gene should look in public), dragged a reluctant Pinn along the promenade before Pinn said, "enough," and dragged the dog, who slipped easily in his boots, to a covered bench out of the wind on the western side of le Jardin Garden fountain.

"Rough," woofed the dog, whose wish was to continue.

Pinn explained he did not feel like struggling into the blizzard but was happy enough to sit for a while under protection and watch what havoc may unfold. Other people, though not many, were still out and about and two ferries were approaching the quay.

Pinn placed his end of the dog leash on the bench beside him, took a cigarette from his holder, and was about to light it when Gene took off at breakneck speed back down the promenade to where a young lady had just turned the corner. Pinn stood, yelled, and began to chase but soon realized there was no way he could catch or influence the belligerent mongrel. He kept walking at pace. He hoped the dog was not going to harm the young lady.

He didn't. It was almost like watching a cartoon. About five meters before he reached the girl, the dog stopped running, leaned back, and skated forward on all fours for a few meters. Composing himself as he slowed and stopped, he formally bowed (stretched), then sat, ears erect, at a right angle to her approach. She said something as she walked past and the dog fell into step beside her.

"You seem to know the dog," said Pinn as the girl approached.

"I do," she said walking past. "He looks ridiculous."

Pinn was forced to about face and jog briefly before he could fall into step with her too.

"How," he asked when he caught up?

"The boots for a start."

"No. I meant how do you know the dog?"

"My mother gave him to that girl, your babysitter, Renée I think. You are Pinn are you not," she asked stopping? "You look like the pictures in the paper."

"I am."

"Sit," she said.

They were back at the bench near the fountain.

"Why?"

"Why not?"

"Why did your mother give Renée the dog?"

"To get you here today, mostly."

Pinn had nothing to say to that.

The girl introduced herself as Hermine. She was short and slender and casually well rugged for the weather. She wore her dark hair in full curly pigtails. Her eyes were hazel, and her voice was bright. She had a neat nose, wore crimson lipstick, and was very attractive despite, or in spite of excessive jewelry.

It left Pinn dithery and time passed during which Hermine didn't seem the least bit uncomfortable. She petted the dog.

Collecting himself Pinn asked, "why here, today?"

"To give you this," she smiled, delving into a bag she had slung over her shoulder.

Except for the cover, which was printed in Atarlia expansive 36, it looked like a photocopied manual of something for beginners. Its title, *Treatise on the Great Red Spot* rang no bells for Pinn.

"That might be the why and here," said Pinn taking the slim volume, "but what about today?"

"Good to see you are paying attention," said Hermine. "Read the treatise."

She stood and offered Pinn her hand.

Pinn stood and accepted it.

Her walk, as she walked away, reminded him of someone.

*

The Great Red Spot is a curiosity on Jupiter. The treatise, no author, attested The Great Red Spot was much greater in size in days of old, circa the middle of the fifth to the middle of the fourth millennium before the current era, and it was a birth canal, of sorts, for comets. The last being delivered around the time mentioned above.

It further attested that the comet, mothered by Jupiter, bounced off the Earth's atmosphere a few years after birth, changing both bodies orientation. It returned after a time and did the same thing again but on a smaller scale before scudding off to find its own elliptic and evolve into a planet. Venus. A couple of stoushes with Mars a few centuries later tidied up her orbit.

Whoever wrote the treatise cleverly employed the Bible to support its claims. It used Exodus and the Conquest to demonstrate its collision theory. The author's Jupiter and other astronomical information however, was unsupported except by a dubious and damaged clay tablet, EA-36972, found at Sippar in 1876, by the Engel's archaeological team. What there was of it was translated twenty-seven years later by Engel's partner's son, Crusdapple Kreme, who, being somewhat egocentric, epilogued it with his uniquely fantastical views. Most of which the treatise endorsed.

Summarizing, the author suggested that Jupiter is getting ready to deliver another baby.

Pinn thought the work a quirky read but he knew nothing about such things.

Three weeks later, a cool but sunny morning, Hermine turned up again. She was waiting on the bench at the garden gate. Pinn had to let go of the dog's leash a good distance away lest he be dragged to her on his face and hands. As he approached, she rose and began to walk at a pace Pinn could easily match.

She wore a short tartan skirt, calf-high boots, and a scrubbed version, in green, of a denim jacket with rhinestones and cowgirl trills. She still had fluffy pigtails and that same shoulder bag was there occasionally bouncing off her thigh. She handed Pinn the dog leash she'd detached, then pocketed her hands.

The three walked side by side, Hermine in the middle.

"So, what did you think," she asked?

Looking down, Pinn swizzled his leading toe for a few steps before answering.

"To be honest Hermine, I'm not a Sci-Fi sort of guy. The yarn was good. It read like whoever wrote it knew what they were talking about. On purely layman's terms, when it came to proof, the millennia stuff was iffy, the biblical support iffier, all conspiracy theorists use the bible. Other things were less iffy, but Ramone seems to be on your side."

"Meaning?"

"She said the tale was allegorical, burley, bait."

"Meaning?"

"I did a little research. The evidence supporting Jupiter being the birth mother of comets or a comet is scant. However, there are many stories relating to Venus. There are those that purport to show her non presence not more than six thousand years ago. Others, many others tell of a contest between Earth and a comet thirteen hundred years later during which the comet, over the following centuries becomes a planet.

Then there is the whole Tiamat thing, the planet of crossing, which adds hundreds of thousands of years to the timeline and sheds a whole different light on the matter. The time difference is significant between the two theories, yet both use the bible in their arguments. Confusing."

Hermine said nothing. They walked on.

Pinn became locked in museful strides but after a while looked up and remembered he was in company. To the right was a bench. He suggested they sit.

Hermine lit a cigarette and ruffled the dog's ears.

Pinn, too, found a cigarette.

He went on. "Should what is implied in the treatise begin now, a cosmic event brought on by Jupiter deploying another comet, the result here on earth, if it were to fit with alleged past scenarios, would not eventuate in my lifetime."

Hermine dove into her bag and pulled out a small handbook entitled *A Guide for the Perplexed*, translated into English by Isin Nergal, circa -1969.

"This may help," she said.

It didn't.

14.

Oppressed by the pandemic, the treatise, and certain dooms day films, Pinn began to consider how difficult it might be to build a citadel that could support a population of one hundred people for twenty years, meet the population's needs; food, water, waste, power, recreation, etc., where limited support from the environment could be expected, and be strong enough to stand up to or repel whatever force was thrown at it either terrestrially or celestially.

It became an obsession and made Pinn a recluse. When he was not at Cubus working on the problem, which was often, he wandered around the house like a zombie. He didn't wear his rings and he gave up shaving and washing regularly. There was no presence in his conversation, no awareness in his countenance. Everybody avoided him. Even Ramone.

Unfortunately, or maybe fortunately, Pinn was not able to satisfy the brief. Despite coming up with a staggering array of systems to support his deep underground and above ground model, his project turned out to be more of an atrophying Shangri-La than a thriving strong hold.

As with Shangri-La, Pinn began with a fictional location, a three square kilometer flat surface in an engineering program. He designed a two third scale replica of the eight sided pyramid (97.67 meters in height) lined with white lime stone and topped with a gold pyramidion. Aligned true north, Pinn's model was able to collect an exceptional amount of solar energy and store it in the surprisingly efficient organic battery the pyramid housed. He positioned it on the plateau's furthermost end.

As well as lighting everything and powering certain other things, the pyramid also conditioned the air in the underground quarters. It was exhaust driven. As excess heat built up in the pyramid, it sucked fresh air into the complex's increasingly complicated structure via ducts and ultimately to itself. Twelve, twenty meter high structures with voluminous air intake capacity were set strategically on the perimeter of Pinn's plateau.

The delicacy in the balance of the closed environment regarding the healthy sustenance of the human population it would support came when meat – chicken, lamb, beef, pork, milk, cheese, eggs, were weighed against a singularly plant based diet, which was easier to manage and took up much less space by comparison in terms of production. But, as the age old adage goes, the libido eats meat. Pinn factored animals into his equation.

He tried several strategies. None reached the twenty-year sustainability goal. Modeling showed the best he could do for one hundred souls was keep them alive six years as strict, stringy, and sexless vegans, or four, maybe four and a half years as productive meat lovers. In both cases, it was cruel. To everybody's relief, Pinn abandoned the project and went back to his day job.

15.

On Friday, October 11, 2024, Pinn was ready. For what, he didn't know, but he was ready nevertheless. For someone with the level of skepticism he professed to hold regarding a foretold future about to fruit, he surely presented as a believer on that morning.

Pinn physically removed his rings the night before, before laying himself down to a restless and unrewarding sleep. He tossed and turned all night long and only sank into a deep and satisfying slumber five minutes before he was woken.

His strategy for the day was to follow his exact routine, and not waver unless forced. On a Friday morning, his routine started with a walk along the promenade.

Gene was not waiting by the car with Gustaf when Pinn arrived.

"Where is he," Pinn asked?

Gustaf shrugged.

After a while, Pinn shrugged too, got into the car and drove off.

He wore a calf length heavy, dark, unbuttoned coat over boots, jeans, and an appropriate shirt. With an appropriate hat, he could have been a cowboy.

Pinn parked in a convenient place and made his way to the quay. His hands were pocketed in his coat and his step was undecidedly ambulatory until he noticed a ferry was just tying up. He added haste. He did not want to get caught by Gosh Shore who was always on the 6:45 from Saint-Gingolph.

Once past the path the commuters took to their places of work, Pinn slowed. A short distance ahead, gazing out over the lake was a tall fellow dressed like a lumberjack. Pinn veered to his right. Thought he might sit on the bench by the garden.

Pinn saw the big guy approach and take a seat next to him but paid him no mind when he did.

"You're expecting me," the big fellow said eventually.

"No, I'm not," said Pinn. "I'm just sitting here minding my own business. So should you."

It was a fine autumn morning, still brisk. Neither moved much on the bench. Both looked lakeward, legs outstretched, hands pocketed in jeans.

"Finally," said the OyOyann, "assimilation at last. No recollection of any other existence except this one."

Pinn stood as if to leave but found himself seated again. He tried it for a second time. Same result.

"Let's walk," said the OyOyann.

Pinn complied.

"I am going to describe a complicated scenario Pinn," the OyOyann said as they set off at a hands repocketed pace away from the quay. "I will be brief, so pay attention."

"Emerging from the apparition after Mar's conjunction with the sun around 2026, it will become apparent Venus, for whatever reason, has begun to behave erratically regarding its orbit. I don't know the math. Then, at the end of April 2029 when the sun, Mercury, and Saturn are supposed to line up with Venus, a further change to her orbit occurs, which will bring it into a collision course with Earth twenty-two months later. February 2031. More an atmospheric graze than a collision really, but catastrophic enough for you guys. We need you to build an ark, Pinn."

The boys walked on.

"I've been trying to convince myself you were sent by Hermine," said Pinn. "Good joke if you were, but you haven't mentioned Jupiter once."

"Hermine was sent by us," said the OyOyann. "For years now you have been told this day would be special. I am what is special about it."

"A boastful lumberjack."

"An OyOyann actually." They stopped walking. "My name is Bruce. I am to be your facilitator."

"Facilitator?"

"Yes, you will need one."

"Only if I decide to build an ark."

The OyOyann handed Pinn a small onyx, gold tipped rod no bigger than a toothpick with a mysterious white ring at one end.

"What's this," he asked holding it up, only vaguely curious?

"The key to the universe."

"Really."

"No, but it's the next best thing. Zi for seven *shar*."

"I don't want it," said Pinn trying to hand it back. "What's a *shar*?"

"Three thousand, six hundred years. It has to be inserted," said the OyOyann, not taking it.

"Into what," asked Pinn?

"Your cerebellum."

"I definitely don't want it," said Pinn.

"It is too late," the OyOyann went on, "as you already know, you have been chosen."

"No, I don't know," said Pinn. "Chosen for what, and by whom?"

"Genetics. Back in the day when the second and third chromosome were fused to adjust consciousness to breed a slightly brighter race so the higher would not have to be so involved in the day to day running of the place, they went slightly beyond. Long story short, all that time ago, your great grandfather, quite a few thousand years removed, during those procedures, was one of only one who was given the amino acid, *Zeta*-E- methylamino -*A*-alanine-L (ZEAL). It's in your gene pool but is not switched on and will not be until a certain chaos is reached. Our analysts recently discovered that by then it will be too late. Not by much, but too late nonetheless. Hence the intervention."

"What good is *Zeta*-E- methylamino -*A*-alanine-L (ZEAL)?"

"It gives you added megalomania in a pack preservation sort of way and some additional immunities. With your Zi you will walk, for a time, in the realm of the immortals."

"If insertion occurs, I will be stuck, no pun intended, in the scenario you are expounding and a life of subservience."

"Not quite, but it could be worse."

"How?"

"You could die along with everybody else. This time, it, the wrath of God event, will be a fire and a water cleansing.

Your Zi puts you in touch with everything about to follow. Every eventuality and all possible consequences. I cannot tell you much, you have to make the measurements yourself, but you only need sixty well chosen folks and five years."

"Feels like fantasy to me," said Pinn walking on.

"Insert the stick," said the OyOyann, "catch up. It will save us a lot of time. Push it up into the middle of your cerebellum with your thumb. It will slip between the two orbs. I assure you it won't hurt, no air will get in, no blood will escape, and you will find the answers you seek."

"I can't have it turned into a ring," Pinn asked?

"No."

Pinn found a way to excuse himself and went home. The OyOyann chose not to feel insulted by the rashness of the human and allowed Pinn to leave. "Same time, same place tomorrow," he shouted after him.

*

Pinn went to his rooms to collect his rings. Only Snake was showing any interest in contacting him. He passed no one on his way to Cubus but once there put the place into full stealth mode which included a total lockdown. "No calls, no interruptions," Pinn said to Ramone. He made himself a large mocha and went to recline on the day bed that looked out over the lake and part of the shore. He adjusted the shade of the dome to keep the sunlight nurturing, rolled a cigarette, lit it, and settled back.

Thanks to the odd white ring attached to the gold tipped toothpick, Pinn put it on his right ring finger with the titanium sup ring. It did not fit tightly, and he could swing the rod from it and fiddle with it, which he did.

Pinn was prepared to believe the OyOyann was the event that was supposed to happen on the day. There was a familiarity about the encounter. But he didn't like the implication of hard work and inconvenience to follow. Inconvenience particularly. Outliving a celestial event was not something someone plans to attempt at the age of forty-five.

"I see you have been given the key to the universe," said Ramone appearing unexpectedly, "will you be getting a Mu and a Shem too?"

"I don't know what they are," said Pinn dropping his hand to his lap. "It's my Zi. Whatever that is, twenty five thousand, two hundred years' worth of it. Supposedly. How did you know what it was?"

"It has to be inserted," said Ramone.

"I know. But how do you?"

"Would you like me to do it?"

"You are a hologram, said Pinn, "you can't."

Ramone took offense to that and left for a few minutes.

Pinn could feel her return before he could see her. The scent of patchouli filled the air and the light changed from natural to artificial. There may have been sitars playing.

It was an odd encounter. On the one occasion Pinn spoke about it, he treated it as if it were a dream and he was not responsible. Like on so many other occasions.

Ramone was dressed unusually alluringly. All pink, playful and suggestive. She sat at the end of the day bed. She told Pinn his Zi would allow her to become matter as opposed to light and was willing to demonstrate. Pinn pretended to fling the key to her, and she pretended to catch it. From the foot of the day bed, she slowly crawled over the reclined Pinn, big cat like. She made sure he could see every curve and cleavage as she did.

Normally, Ramone exuded no presence beyond her capable mind, words, and what she was wearing – how she looked. Differently, on this occasion, perhaps because she was wearing little clothing and had perfumed the air, a silent, even menacing presence grew stronger the closer she came to meeting Pinn's eyes. When she did, she positioned her womanhood above Pinn's interested manhood. Pinn got comfortable. Forgetting the toothpick, he clasped his hands behind his head placing his Zi, unwittingly, in an almost perfect position for insertion. All it needed was a little push. Somehow, Ramone performed it. There was an immense surge of incoming power through Pinn's cranium followed almost immediately by a similar surge of outgoing energy lower down, which Ramone rode all the way to the end. The whole thing lasted fifteen seconds.

The rules exclude a cyberphon, Ramone, from completing an insertion so it, the Zi, only stayed in place briefly. She did well however. She felt seeded, which is what she wanted. Both fell asleep after the brief but intense event. Ramone, still with a residual body weight, atop Pinn.

The Global Daze network, worldwide, went down during those fifteen seconds. Snake and Grubb were expecting something to happen on a system level due to the significance of the day for Pinn, but they weren't expecting a total outage. After isolating Cubus, something never done before, they had the rest of the system up again in twenty seven minutes, Cubus thirty minutes later. But Cubus remained in lock down.

Nellie contacted Snake during the outage. All he could tell her before talking to Pinn was that it was October 11, 2024, the date Ramone and the muses had made ominous for Pinn for nearly eight years. It was the day on which Pinn had somehow, contrary to popular opinion, come to believe he may perish. "And he may have", said Snake. "Cubus is in a total lockdown and, though perfectly functional, has been quiet now for over three hours. The only way to rescind the lockdown without Pinn's consent requires a protocol Ramone alone can instigate and she, unexplainably, can't be raised. Hence, nor can Pinn."

"So, what are you going to do?"

"Nothing," said Snake, "Pinn does not get killed or even hurt today. When I question Mia or any of the other muses about the day, what they report is gibberish, but it is obvious Pinn remains alive."

"Did you ask Ramone?"

"No, you know what Ramone would say."

"Then if you know nothing, but think everything will be all right, I'm off to play Bridge," said Nell.

"I don't, yes, do. I'll be in touch," finished Snake.

*

Notwithstanding the rule excluding a cyberphon from completing an insertion, the other rules in relation to the Zi were basic. Self-insertion was easiest but someone one could seed was preferred if one needed help.

When Michelle returned to her rooms that afternoon after her usual stint at the squash court with the children, she found Ramone glowing whitely on the divan. Ramone and she developed a relationship after Nell asked Pinn to get Ramone to get Miss Trust to talk to her.

"You look pale," said Michelle. "Is that intended?"

Ramone told Michelle Pinn had just received the key to the universe but was reluctant to accept it.

What Michelle really wanted to do was take a hot bubble bath and chill. She had always worried about Pinn's naivete. Now she was wondering about Ramone's as well. Who could bestow such a thing on a person and why Pinn she thought? A question she repeated to Ramone.

Ramone told Michelle about ZEAL, about the impending global catastrophe, and about Pinn being offered the key to the universe. Michelle stifled her skepticism until Ramone produced it, the key, the Zi, the gold tipped onyx toothpick on a mysterious white ring. Doubt changed to interest.

Ramone borrowed it from the sleeping Pinn to help her to convince Michelle to insert it. Michelle asked why Ramone was so adamant it should be inserted. Ramone told her it was her duty to protect her protector and that she was with child.

Michelle found that ludicrous. Holograms, even with synced intelligence, as a rule, cannot carry anything let alone a child.

Dangling by the mysterious white ring, Ramone extended Pinn's Zi toward Michelle on the pointed forefinger of her red right hand. She dared Michelle to take it.

Michelle did, and with a touch, all her questions were answered. The Zi made it clear what she had to do and why she should do it.

Michelle took her bubble bath and chilled. Cubus remained silent and in lockdown. Ramone set permissions to allow Michelle to enter Cubus.

*

It was nearly dark when Michelle arrived at Cubus to find Pinn still asleep on the day bed.

Rather than wake Pinn directly, Michelle decided to clatter around as best she could in her automated world getting a glass of champagne for herself and a boiler maker for Pinn. It worked.

"I just woke," said Pinn sitting up as Michelle placed his drinks on the coffee table next to him.

"It's past cocktail hour darling," said Michelle. "Can you not use a drink? It looks like you have had a tough day."

Pinn took that with the wry intended.

"Did you know ReadMe went down today during your little frolic with Ramone," she continued, "and that Cubus has been blacked out now for more than six hours?"

"What frolic, is ReadMe up?"

"Yes, the system is up again. It took Snake and the Grub about half an hour to fully restore it. The disruption came from Cubus, which they intuitively suspected and which took time to isolate since it had never been done before. But once it was, ReadMe popped back up again with only a little wear and tear on certain hubs. When they got back to bringing Cubus online again it seemed whatever caused the problem had passed so it was reconnected, but not before coding in a master kill switch should the situation ever arise again."

"Ramone let them do that," asked Pinn?

"Ramone reckons she's pregnant," said Michelle.

"Seems a stretch," said Pinn.

"Indeed," said Michelle. "What's this," she asked, holding up Pinn's Zi by the mysterious white ring?

Pinn checked the finger where he thought his Zi ought to be.

"How did you get that," he asked?

"Ramone gave it to me. How does a hologram carry something physical?"

"It doesn't."

"Yet, I have it."

"You could have taken it from me as I slept."

Pinn told Michelle about the OyOyann, his alleged genetic engineering, the global threat, and that he could save the species from extinction, wasting thousands of years in development, by seeing a growable population through the catastrophe. All he had to do to accomplish that was to insert the thing she held in her hand into his head.

"What are you going to do," asked Michelle taking a seat at the other end of the day bed, "insert it?"

"It's not my first inclination," said Pinn. "You know I am not a big believer in deities or predictions, though I have built a reasonable business from promoting both. But I am not one hundred percent sure that that was free willingly, or actually, my doing, which, if true, suggests a puppet master and my options are two. Live in the world of their creation or die."

"Isn't that what we are doing now?

"They expect me to lead a small group of people through a foreseeable, to them, global cataclysm."

"And if successful, you become a king."

"If successful, I become a schmuck. I imagine it takes decades, maybe even centuries for a planet to reorientate after being struck by a large celestial object. I am not capable of managing that. And why would I want to anyway? I'm having trouble getting through the years I'm already living. What they reckon is a blessing sounds like hell to me.

"Up until this point my life has been gifted. Not because I am particularly bright but rather because circumstance has favored me. I have done very little but at every turn, someone new popped up to prop me up and facilitate my ability to take the next turn. In a closed environment that wouldn't happen."

"This, is the next turn. Don't be so hard on yourself. Would you like me to do it?"

"Do what?"

"Insert it, your Zi," she said, sidling toward Pinn one wiggle at a time until she was almost against him.

Pinned turned to face her, and just as he was about to answer, Michelle cupped her hands behind his neck in a loving gesture and kissed him gently as she inserted the toothpick into Pinn's skull. Michelle said the thing seemed to get sucked right in as soon as it got close to the spot where it was supposed to go.

Though Pinn experienced the same sort of sensation as he did the first time he was pierced by his Zi, Michelle did not fall pregnant from the kiss.

16.

The following day started ordinarily enough, Pinn met up with the OyOyann around 7:30 am and they walked. There was a brisk breeze and a crisp light, and their banter was jovial. The OyOyann was pleased the insertion had been completed successfully. Pinn remained bashful about the subject.

At the end of the promenade, there was a gazebo Pinn had never noticed before. The OyOyann suggested they sit. There were formalities to conclude. They took seats on opposite sides of the sheltered table.

"Unfortunately for you," said the OyOyann, "you are not Noah. He had seven days warning. There was subterfuge and deviousness, but he got the job done. His project was a little smaller. You, on the other hand, have a little over six years' warning, which makes your job considerably more complicated.

"This time around Pinn you don't get three chances like you did the first time, you have to get it in one.

"What first time?"

"Five years from now, in 2029, there will be considerable worldly chaos once the news gets out about what the solar system has in store for Earth.

"Three years ago, we took advantage of a certain alignment in the stars to install a large underground facility which, I believe, will withstand the pressures the planet will face during the time of the clash. It is in a remote location in central Australia. But before anything can happen there the land above it needs to be leased so we can build an appropriate above-ground transition platform."

"I thought you said I had to build the ark?"

"The technology does not exist on earth to build a suitable structure for the job. I forgot the species was behind schedule intellectually. But, once you have access to our installation, which you should be able to make happen in the next few months, the obligation is the same. You must fill its accommodations and storage, manage its processes and promote production while steering the vessel through unchartered territory. The success or failure of the endeavor will still fall to you."

Bruce waited while Pinn, who hadn't shaved in a few days, scratched his stubble, and mulled that over before standing and making as if to leave.

"Look," he said, "it might not be easy but it's doable. Your Zi will confirm it.

"For the past three hours, unbeknownst to you, we have been flitting to various places in the universe to feed you, subliminally, the copious volumes of information needed for the step you are about to take. When your Zi gives immortality to your current mortality, a certain brainial infrastructure has to be in place to fortify the otherwise underutilized organ.

"You already know all you need to know. You just have to learn how to access it."

"How do I access it," asked Pinn.

"Moon the noon sun in about three minutes from now," said the OyOyann.

"Fun knee," said Pinn. "You do it."

"Did I say I was leaving," Bruce asked?

"I am leaving," he confirmed. "I am expected in the Turso nebula at a planet called Goosel. They have a nourishment and intoxicants festival there every shar that should not be missed. I will be gone twenty-eight days in your time."

"What do I do until then?"

"Get in contact with your Zi."

"How do I do that?"

"Since you have missed the easy noon moon option, think about how it started for you Earthling. Consciousness, sustenance, hierarchy. What came first?

"Thanks,' said Pinn, 'for nothing."

"My pleasure," said Bruce as he disappeared into the midday sun.

Part Three

Fate

1.

They called themselves gods, they were self-proclaimed. They did have a lot to back it up, but Pinn still reckoned it was just a time and space thing. They were taller, but they still looked human. Their universe was bigger, maybe considerably bigger and everything just expanded out from there. The title, God, was meant to inspire awe in the lulus they gave it to, and it did. But there is still no infinity, just a longer timeline. It was not inconceivable to Pinn that the OyOyann knew people who called themselves Gods too.

On the morning of November 6, 2024, a Wednesday, the day after he returned from the Turso nebula, Bruce woke Pinn from a sound sleep just after 3 a.m. The unexpectedly being woken kerfuffle was the same as usual.

"Where are we going," asked Pinn, hopping and skipping down the arcade, trying to keep up with the stride of the OyOyann as they made their way to the elevators to Cubus?

"You have an appointment," said Bruce brightly.

"So early, I haven't had coffee."

"Coffee will be available," Bruce continued as the elevator began to rise, "along with pastries, fruit, finger sandwiches, a small selection of hot nibblies, and cigarettes. The gods don't usually smoke but since you do, on this occasion, it will be permitted.

"Considerate," said Pinn.

"We'll see," said Bruce.

The elevator journey seemed long to Pinn, and he was just about to comment on it when it stopped and he found himself standing alone, not in Cubus but in a large hall garishly clad in gold, red velvet, and shadows. There was a murmur coming from a small group gathered some distance away. Since nobody came for him, Pinn approached.

When he neared, his presence had no effect on the dynamics of the group, so he went to the buffet where there was a coffee awaiting him. It was in a black, 12oz takeaway cup with his initials on it. It had a white spout lid and was just how he liked it. Hot, white, and sweet.

He found the cigarettes at a table nearby, then sat on the lounge seat provided to smoke one. They were those excellent Longfellows. He tried to tune into the conversation, but it was hard. The participants were about twenty feet away, the language may have been different, and they did not speak loudly often.

However, as he observed the discussion, Pinn came up with monikers for the three: He who does not speak much, the stern administrator, and the doer. The doer turned out to be Bruce. Pinn didn't recognize him at first because he wasn't dressed in his usual lumberjack garb.

Pinn had finished his cigarette and nodded off by the time the trio finally approached. Bruce kicked a protruding foot to wake him.

"This is who you have chosen to survive the apocalypse, said the stern administrator to the doer, Bruce, as Pinn got to his feet.

"Yes," said Bruce.

"Supports my view it's a waste of time," said the stern administrator.

"How?" questioned Pinn without thinking.

The stern administrator looked Pinn up and down, chose a honeyed fig and camembert croissant from the buffet, and poked it skyward before pulling it down. The croissant was used frequently during the ensuing speech to make certain points but at no time did it ever go anywhere near the stern administrator's mouth. And in the end, it was just gone.

"I was against it from the beginning," he began, "but father intervened on the side of the mutineers and so I ceded. It delayed things a little as far as my plans were concerned, as the species was developed, but once the hybrid was up and running, things went well for a while. But then, like those before them, the birthmothers mutinied. So, then the question became about whether, or whether not to enable procreation in the species. I was against that too for the obvious reasons, but, as usual, Bruce, contrary to council consensus, went ahead and did it anyway. So, if you want someone to blame for your current predicament Earthling, blame Bruce. Who do you think the snake was in the Garden of Eden? And why did he want you to know anyway? To get back on point, the planet is almost depleted of resources for the time being and the population is a little too impolite for me. I see no reason to interfere with fate."

"Fate is subjective brother," said Bruce.

"He's your brother," queried Pinn?

"Yes, and that's my father," he said, nodding in the direction of he who does not speak much.

An argument occurred between the two brothers. The stern administrator wanted to close the book on Earth due to the pending disturbance and walk away. It was low on their preferred supplier list anyway, and anything Earth had they could get elsewhere.

The doer agreed to disagree, said the investment he had put into the place had been substantial in terms of the being being created, quite a few thousand years in fact, and he wanted to see it out.

Here the language changed. It was pointedly rhythmic and syllabic at first. Pinn didn't understand a word of it, but he did notice as the volume increased toward the end, the surprising amount of venom one could spit from a vowel, and the threat and disdain a consonant could carry.

He who does not speak much held up his hand and the brothers stopped. He brought it down on the side of Bruce and the matter was decided.

*

After a round of strong drinks to celebrate, he who does not speak much left, and the stern administrator got down to business.

"In 2021, when we sent Hermine to see you, it was still undecided whether the planet's human species should be saved. Optimistic Bruce thought it should since some were his handy work. He built an elaborate underground facility capable of supporting sixty or so people, other life, their needs, and ours through the worst of the pending upheaval. As of a few moments ago, the facility was gifted to you. All you have to do to gain access Earthling, is lease the land above our site and allow Bruce to install the necessary infrastructure.

"There is no guarantee of survival of course," he went on. "According to my vague understanding of the event, so much electrical energy will be generated by Venus's approach that forty percent of the globe will frizzle. When Venus touches down or comes as close to it as it is going to, a tsunami of great might will grow up in the middle of your Pacific Ocean. You will be among the first to experience its wrath."

The stern administrator seemed quite happy about all that, nodded at his brother and walked off. But before he disappeared into the darkness he turned to Pinn and wished him luck.

"Sounds like fun," said Pinn after he departed.

"I told you," said Bruce.

Pinn lit another cigarette and found a new cup of coffee with his initials on it on the table.

"When you mentioned you wanted to see it out," said Pinn, "you and your brother changed to another language and got quite worked up in the end. What was that all about?"

"A long way from now, Earthling. You have to survive a flood and a holocaust first. Or vice versa. And then there is the final hurdle."

Pinn didn't ask what the final hurdle was, too much had already been promised.

2.

Pinn's initial request to lease the parcel of land above the OyOyann facility from the owners of the remote property in central Australia received a flat no. But a few weeks later at the dinner table, the patriarch mentioned to his son that he had received an offer to lease some land near where the dry rivers meet. His son then related an unusual event.

A little over three years earlier, the son told how, for a week, he commuted by helicopter to Unn Well, about a hundred and fifty kilometers southeast of the homestead. A freak storm had bent the shaft of the windmill there and torn a number of blades off its face. It was a big job for one person but by the end of the week, he managed to repair it and get it back up and running. From the beginning, as the days passed, he grew increasingly ill. By Friday noon, he had a spectacular fever and had begun to hallucinate. After making a final check of the apparatus with Bob, a small bloke with a big spanner who accompanied him everywhere and said okay to everything, he got into the helicopter to fly home. He realized he probably should not be flying but he did not want to spend the night there. Bob would not get into the chopper with him. He took off alone. All he had to do, he told himself, was stay high enough and fly a smidge right into the setting sun.

It was hard going, and he struggled all the way. It was November 12, 2021. He remembered the date because it was his Bonsaied maple, Sarah's, sixteenth birthday and he had planned to give her a little trim and a few grains of sugar after dinner that night. He had been looking forward to it all week.

About an hour out from the homestead he noticed he was flying slightly further north than he ought. It took him a little while to figure out why. A sun like orb seemed to shadow, if that's the right word, the sun itself, only higher and right. The son put the second sun down to his hallucinations and adjusted his course. In the following thirty minutes, the second sun overtook the first sun and made contact with the earth just near where the two rivers meet. There was no impact. when the orb touched down it was simply absorbed perpendicularly. He could see ground zero glowing off to his left as he flew past. He said he didn't say anything about it at the time because of the hallucinations. When he flew by the site a couple of days later, everything seemed normal. Mentioning the dry rivers brought the memory back.

The patriarch had lived most of his eighty-four years out in open land and rarely left it. He had seen much go on in the night sky and had developed a personal theory about extra-terrestrials long ago. Most knew that about the patriarch, so none were surprised when he reversed his decision and leased the land after hearing his son's tale. "If the aliens are here," he said, "I want to meet them."

Pinn said he could not promise aliens but thanked the patriarch for allowing the lease to proceed, and invited him to visit anytime.

3.

One of the first things Pin did when he realized he had to talk to everybody about an ark, was ask Snake and Stheno to come to Cubus to discuss adjusting an unused application in the ReadMe suite. It was called Voya, and it could be found way down the index with all the other V's. What it did was capture every living second of the life of the subscriber, if turned on. What Pinn wanted it to do was monitor every living second of the lives of several subscribers, prod them if they strayed off the preferred line, put words into their mouth if they were about to disclose something disadvantageous to the endeavor, and finally, incapacitate them if they failed to comply.

Stheno thought that was fair enough.

"A lot of work," said Snake.

"I have an idea," said Pinn.

"You wouldn't have called if you didn't."

"The muses. We are only going to be monitoring twenty or thirty people at the outset. Family and friends. If we allow the muses to run freely amongst the groups' data and keep an eye on them at the same time, we will know all we need to know, or the machine will, and with a few parameters we will stop anything from getting out."

Snake wondered what could get out. Nevertheless, if that's what Pinn wanted that's what Pinn would get. Using the muses made the task simpler. But, he added, he would not be able to put words into a person's mouth, change what they are going to say, so to speak. So, whatever they are going to say, they will, in fact, say.

Pinn was not happy with that. After a moment's ponderance, he said, "we will electrocute them. We have the capacity to send a charge to any implant or accessory on our system, if someone is going to say something, write something, or type something we don't like, we will electrocute them while they are trying to do it and stop when they are not. Mia will love it."

"A bit brutal, Pinn," said Snake. "Electrocution. I thought you said the program was for family and friends."

"It is."

Snake sent the finished code to Pinn a couple of days later. It required a chip modification for maximum effect. Pinn had Ramone enter the parameters and enrolled the first participants.

Pinn didn't think the electrocution part would be much of a problem, but Catherine got shocked almost immediately after the system went live.

4.

Bruce named the site Petalgeuse.

The structure was simple; it was the large aforementioned sphere observed by the patriarch's son, nine kilometers in diameter, buried underground, wearing a six square kilometer andesite and granite slab hat. Bruce installed a low-rise resort-style facility at the eastern end of the slab near where the rivers met. Access to the sphere from the above-ground structures was through tunnels carved into the bedrock and transfer stations.

"How do I tell the story of pending doom and get anybody to believe me," asked Pinn? "What do I say to Nell,

Catherine, Renée, Justine, Izabella, Snake, the Grubb, Dip, Stheno, Gustaf, Greta, Brittany, and Smitten to convince them that what I am saying will eventuate and the only way to survive is to form an enterprise of believers? If I cannot convince them, I will have to kill them."

"With expanded technology comes an exubjugant in the psychology of the species to which the technology was granted," said Bruce. "It's one of those quirks that allows the shifter, for a short time, to be unlikely."

"Meaning what?"

"Meaning we will orientate your family and friends for you. We are set up to do it and we should get on with it. Time is of the essence."

Pinn and Bruce were sitting on a bench in the shade by Petalgeuse's pool looking past it and out into the barrenness. They had spent the last couple of hours touring the underground. Pinn was feeling overwhelmed.

"Are you aware, or do you have any insight into what the final outcome might be, where we humans are concerned," asked Pinn?

"None," chirped Bruce. "Not at your level. That's what you're Zi is for Pinn. But we have a very good idea about what will happen to the planet generally and there are some things about its condition after the worst of it has passed which lead us to believe you can prevail."

"Like what?"

"The atmosphere survives. It gets a little murky and will stay that way for a long time but, hopefully, it's something you can manage."

"How?"

"Unlike Moses who wandered around above ground in the remnants for years, you get to do it more like Captain Lemo, below ground, in the vessel on which we sit."

"It would be nice, Bruce," said Pinn, "if you sometimes spoke Earthlian."

"Petalgeuse, the ark of your inheritance, the subterranean structure we built for you to survive the cataclysm.

"Petalgeuse has the capacity to filter its atmosphere. It is two spheres, one inside the other where the smaller sphere is cushioned from the protective outer shell by a potable water moat under pressure. The smaller of the spheres (seven kilometers in diameter) is where the facilities are built, and from calculations we have made, the outer shell should be able to protect the inner sphere from any heat or pressure imposed, but it's not guaranteed.

"As you just saw, it has everything, an eco-system where you can grow grains and vegetables, fruit and fowl, cows and sows. It has living quarters with all the usual amenities in a village setting, with a town square and a clock. It has a bridge for the captain, well equipped offices and laboratories, and, best of all, if the orb loses its hat, a gyroscope at its heart will keep the sphere in which you live, perfectly stable. But again, there is no guarantee."

"No guarantee twice sounds heartless Bruce."

"You heard my brother," replied Bruce, "did he sound like he had a heart? For you, being so far down the food chain, there are no heavenly favors. If your species becomes extinct, something else will replace it. But having said that, I have a vested interest in this one. You are my creation. Not you personally but the species partially, and I hold certain ambitions regarding its development which, if you are successful, could see you father a dynasty.

"That was better," said Pinn.

*

Pinn arranged what he called a wellness retreat to Petalgeuse for all family and friends, except the young ones, where Bruce would present the future. He didn't tell anyone about that part, he just said everybody had been working so hard they needed a break, a chance to unwind and catch up with themselves again. There was disgruntlement from Catherine, Snake, and the Grubb but somehow Pinn was able to get them to participate.

He called the break a wellness retreat so nobody would get overly suspicious about the lack of communication with the outside world at the facility - there was none, or think the insistence of the wellness mother, Sugar, to be active was something otherwise contrived. Ride a horse, feed a pig, plant a gorse, do a jig, were some of the suggestions suggested by the personable hostess on arrival. Meet back here at around sunset for a beer or two, a goanna stew, and some damper, was too.

It was a two week retreat and Pinn sent his people to Petalgeuse in small groups of four or five at a time. After a week, as the first group moved underground, the second group flew in to begin as the first group had, in the above ground quarters. It took around two months to get everybody through.

On the first night, most were exhausted by the time they found themselves awaiting their stew. Not because they did anything during the day but because they did nothing. Connectivity withdrawal was a draining experience. All started out by poking their gunja and bush basil-flavored goanna around their bowls with their damper but there was not a skerrick left in the end.

A few days later, when people had settled down, dabbled in some activities, and ate anything put in front of them, even a sweet and crunchy cricket and Goyder bean satay, Sugar asked what they thought the end of the world would look like and if they had the opportunity to save themselves from it along with a few others, would they take it? Responses varied, and questions came up, which Sugar answered with the deft of the Delphinian, Pythia.

Early in the morning of the seventh day, Sugar put herself and her guests in hats and on horseback and set off at a wandering pace into the barrenness. By noon they arrived at a camp site marked by an unusual rock formation. There they had a light lunch before Sugar rose to her feet and said something that sounded very much like, open sesame.

The rock formation split in two to reveal a cave.

The cave led to an elevator; the elevator descended into the underworld. With everybody aboard, Sugar pressed the button.

For the following week guests lived entirely in the underground facility. Their housing was not unlike that above ground.

A quick tour of the site on their first morning there highlighted the astonishing attributes of the facility. There were fields of wheat, patches for vegetables, and a small orchard on one level, pastures of livestock and other animals on another. There was an open office area, a technology bubble, processing plants, laboratories, power generators, storage environments, and much more.

It was a lot to take in and the tour was done quickly on purpose. A big evening lay ahead. Sugar encouraged all to rest up during the afternoon.

After a hearty meal of oxen Stroganoff with pappardelle and a glass or two of chianti around an underground campfire at the town center, the group were taken to New Cubus a few levels below for a meeting with Bruce, where the revelation would be revealed.

This meeting went differently for each group but essentially Bruce introduced himself as Do Er, first born to he who does not speak much, but only second in line to the throne due to a technicality. The associated detail to confirm or deny Bruce's assertions was absent in the group before him but Bruce felt the need to point it out anyway.

With his credentials sufficiently addled, Bruce told everyone to call him Bruce.

"I am going to relate a complicated story," he imparted, "so pay attention."

He described the details of the recently discovered anomalies in Venus's orbital behavior and how it would lead, in seven years' time, to Venus coming close enough to Earth to create an ELE. An extinction level event. Nothing could be done.

It is fair to say news of that sort was entirely unexpected by the group. Stunned bafflement and skepticism was the standard reaction. Bruce enjoyed that part of the evening and saw no reason to rush through it. He would suggest a nice cup of tea and a cookie or two before he continued.

Next came a movie, a short, six-minute time-lapse film of Earth from late 2030 to the end of February 2031, from a Jupiterians eye view, in close-up. Venus approaches Earth, there is a graze, a collision? Earth's axis is visibly altered in the wake of the encounter which looked electrically frightening if nothing else.

When Snake saw the footage, he pointed out it could be a scam. "It's easy enough to produce something like that and call it the future," he said. "We could do it. Inventing the story wouldn't be too hard either." The rest of his group, Grubb, Dip, and Stheno agreed.

Bruce did too but questioned why anyone *would* do it considering the significant consequence it would evoke in the public arena. Violence, and hardship not the least. Snake and the team remained unconvinced by the alien.

For the next six days of orientation, participants were left to their own devices in the underground facility. They were encouraged to roam freely and familiarize themselves with what will become their home and workplace in the near future. Some did it in groups, some did it alone.

Snake and his team found the space where they would set up their servers and met Nice, the OyOyann female responsible for the module. Nice, was one of Bruce's crew. A contingent of twenty four OyOyann tasked with getting Petalgeuse up and running.

Izabella did it alone, and spent most of her time hanging out with Zac, a young OyOyann male who was toiling in a field with his shirt off under a convincingly hot and sunny LED sky, when Izabella first saw him. She was sixteen, Zac was a little less than a hundred thousand. Calculated back into earth years, Zac would have been around nineteen.

As the days passed, everyone seemed to immerse themselves in the spirit of the facility and took to being underground as a matter of course.

There was no certificate or ceremony at the completion of the retreat, but all participants received an upgrade to their ReadMe chip and a leaflet describing the changes. A brief description of the electrocution feature was mentioned on page three of the leaflet, which nobody read at first.

5.

At no time in those first months did Pinn think he knew what he was doing. His Zi knew everything, but it presented too many choices. It made his head ache. Bruce let it be. Pinn toyed through things he thought he should be doing. By 2026 Pinn's head eased.

Venus had begun to creep enough in her orbit to be noticed by some observers on Earth. It didn't seem much, and those who noticed kept it to themselves.

*

One day, out of the blue, Pinn decided Petalgeuse needed a concierge. Frank.

Frank impressed Pinn when he worked with him at a boutique hotel in Perth for a few months around Christmas 2006. They became friends. Frank was the concierge, Pinn was the house chauffeur. Frank knew everything about everyone who ever set foot in the hotel foyer, why they were in town, and what their requirements might be. He was a casual and confidant Italian in his early thirties. His accent had a pinched, swallowed, nasal quality about it. A handsome beak facilitated its rich resonance. He always dressed impeccably, smelt good, and was the best handler of people Pinn had ever witnessed.

Pinn asked Ramone to track him down. She found him in Milan. A hop, skip, and a jump away. A few days later Pinn droned in, called him, said he was in town, and asked if they might catch up. Frank was delighted to hear from Pinn, it had been so many years. "Would you like me to send you some girls," he asked?

Pinn thanked Frank for the offer but declined as he had always done. He said he would like to meet, however, if Frank had the time.

"Of course," said Frank clicking his heels. "It would be my pleasure."

The following day they met at around 2 pm at a quiet Naviglio Grande café. Frank sat upright and sipped an espresso while Pinn smoked, and drank sweet, white tea. Frank sometimes became animated and elaborate of gesture but mostly he listened in still attentiveness.

Pinn skimmed over the Earth catastrophe and alien part of his story quickly and focused on the wellness center he had established in a remote location in central Australia. He expressed his need for a hands-on person at the site who could handle the traffic. As it happened, Frank had just divorced his second wife and was good to go. There were no children from either marriage.

On their way to a nearby tattoo parlor with a qualified body piercer, Frank asked Pinn if it would be possible to find a role for his nephew, his youngest sister's firstborn.

Maybe in security. "He is a good boy," he said. "He was recently discharged from the army.

"Honorably or dishonorably," Pin queried?

"I didn't ask, said Frank"

Jacob was young, twenty-four, and presented with the physique and confidence of good breeding. He had shiny black hair, which he parted slightly left and shinier white teeth, a straight nose, and really red, lubre, lips. Unlike his uncle, he didn't look like he needed to shave every fifteen minutes. He played football in his boy hood, switched to triathlon in his teens, and joined the army later, while he was still in them. Frank said he was in some sort of secret unit.

"Why not," said Pinn?

*

Snake and Stheno had established the mainframe for what would become the child of ReadMe at Petalgeuse. Thus far it was fed via satellite from Glenst Yng and was not yet an entity unto itself. Some of the array was also learning a new way to compute due to the alien protocols of the host machine also called Petalgeuse. Snake pointed this out to Pinn in terms of his conspiracy theory. "It could influence our machine to our detriment," he said, "and we wouldn't know it."

Pinn said, the new way to compute runs the water, power, and waste. Unless it's sending seditious messages to undesirables who listen to audio of its movements played backward, I think we should proceed where necessary with the alien protocol and see what happens."

The children, Sumonus, Atlaseze, and Lilita, eleven, had moved permanently to the site and were being cared for by Greta, Gustaf, Sugar, and Frank, not counting the OyOyann. Renée did not consider herself to be the nursery mother anymore.

It was thought, where the children were concerned, it was better to raise them in the life they will face both environmentally and obstacley in the future rather than the indulgent one in which they previously resided.

6.

It was a little over four years before Venus would wave to Uluru as it flew by.

The ark was a gigantic synthetic environment that was, in above-ground appliances, megalithic. Underground, there was comfortable, village style living. On the floors below, besides the agriculture module with its fields to be plowed and maintained, there were animals to be fed and exercised, processing plants to monitor, and more. Operations that needed operators and workers.

Family and friends equaled about thirty souls, half of what Petalgeuse could support in terms of people but only a third were used to doing any work. Not counting Bruce, twenty four OyOyann maintained Petalgeuse's productivity at that point. An arrangement that would end at dawn, October 31, 2029. With a recommended capacity of sixty, that left about thirty spaces to fill. They needed workers.

*

Ideologically Pinn's Zi presented a slightly blurred wistfulness to future turns and events, which Pinn found unsatisfactory. He mentioned it to Ramone. She said, "so far, its propaganda as opposed to intuition. You need to believe."

Pinn was changing; he liked his plights crisp and his direction clear. He was developing a casual certainness he could make whatever he wanted to happen, happen. He called a meeting of stakeholders to address the personnel issue.

It was a mistake.

Snake, who Zoomed in from Petalgeuse wanted to talk about his scam. He said aliens always had ulterior motives, otherwise, they wouldn't be here.

"But," he stressed, "what if the narrative they are selling us is not the actual story? What if it would be easier for an invading force to vanquish a planet by simply promoting a wrath of God scenario, that will never occur, to a population known to have conflicting, vengeful Gods to which they are all either fervently passionate, or indifferent. As you pointed out, a social collapse engineered to occur at a strategic moment would wipe billions from the population. Then, thanks to the conflict between religions, most of the remaining souls would perish a short time later squabbling amongst themselves about whose god gave them the right to be supreme. It is a cheaper strategy for conquerors and a lot less work. And our time is often not a factor in these things for them."

"How do you come up with that stuff," asked Pinn?

"The Grubb," said Snake.

"Ok," said Pinn, "let's just as bluntly consider it is not a scam. We have to finish getting whatever we need into Petalgeuse without drawing attention to ourselves over the next two and a half years and have it producing everything we will need to sustain ourselves indefinitely, without the help of the OyOyann.

"Soon the world at large will understand what's coming. Others will build bunkers; some will ready to leave the planet. It wouldn't take Space Ecks much. I believe they are already on the verge of launching forty five of their new ET.NU.12 rockets to carry not only the people to populate but the components to build, in the first three years of flight, a self-sustaining super star ship, capable of warp speeds, which, seventy two years from now will reach a secret location they say can support human life.

"Anyway, in a surprisingly short time, an undefeatable chaos will swallow Earth's populations. Everything will collapse all at once; no food, no fuel, no money, no joke. Superior concerns with gold and other commodities will employ armies to defend the bunkers and the spaceports they build. While not gold or commodity shy ourselves, we will not use an army but protect ourselves instead, through stealth and discipline."

"And the help of the OyOyann," added Snake.

Whoever said it was easier for a camel to pass through the eye of a needle than it was for a rich man to pass through the gates of heaven was ill informed.

*

Later that night when Pinn returned to the house, he found Michelle at the kitchen table with a pot of tea and accessories for two. Her hair was down, and she wore a fawn kimono style dressing gown highlighted by a yellow sash and trimming.

Pouring tea for her husband and fixing it just so, she asked how his day went.

"Fine," said Pinn sitting, acknowledging the mug of tea prepared for him.

After a few moments of silence, Michelle suggested they take their teas down to the terrace where Pinn could smoke, and they could gaze upon a waxing moon and Venus.

She took her husband's hand during the brief walk.

When they had settled and after lighting a cigarette for Pinn and handing it to him, she said, "we should move to Petalgeuse."

"Now?"

"Yes. The children are already there. Their parents should be too. I don't understand what the holdup is.

"The way I see it, as long as you don't move there, nobody else will either, and as far as I can gather you are not being all that successful with a hands-off approach."

Pinn stood and walked toward the glass partition. "I have to be readily available to certain people who may wish to contact me," said Pinn, "not hiding in a remote Australian location we are trying to keep secret."

"You have never been readily available to anybody Pinn, but now, thanks to the evolution of an increased presence of air borne disease in our societies, you can zoom in from just about anywhere. And with your resources, you can make it appear as if you are sitting in the chair opposite. You have always wanted to be a tyrant my love. Here's your chance. Be one."

"I don't think I have it in me," said Pinn.

"The electrocution app was a good start," said Michelle, "and you were right about Mia."

Michelle and Pinn would have left it there, but Catherine suddenly arrived. She had been at the meeting earlier that day and had things she wanted to talk about. Michelle made more tea. Catherine fixed herself a drink.

Over the years, Pinn had no idea what Catherine did for a living. He could have looked but he didn't. When Gorm was alive, she said she worked for him and confidentialities applied, but after he died nothing changed. She used curt, obscure sentences if asked about it.

It turns out she was a head-hunter who was paid well for both her discretion and success. She was working for Gorm, her farther, at about the time they met and continued to work with his businesses for many years after his death.

She had just come back from a girlfriend's party and was well primed. The girlfriend had been dumped by a Canadian crooner. It was one of those Fired-Up parties.

From behind Pinn, as she approached, Catherine began to decry how the meeting earlier that day panned out. By the time she was standing in front of him, she was so worked up about it she wanted to kick him in the shins.

The following opinion, after Catherine had taken a few deep breaths, a few steps back, and Pinn had put his feet up, at first addressed the sudden rank difference between herself and her sister. Why did she, Michelle, not have to take the Wellness Retreat for example, but she did not pursue it. She abhorred the allowance of Snake's scam to be freely discussed at the meeting. She was something of a grifter herself and could easily see Snakes point. She thought Pinn's overall performance in winning the argument, true or false, about whether the pending apocalypse was a hoax or not, poor. "You seem to have no plan and the way the OyOyann tell it, it is too late to turn back. But you have hired a concierge and his nephew."

"Yes. Frank. Have you met him?"

"No."

She then presented evidence she had been paying attention at the meeting and at the Wellness Retreat and began to outline how she would proceed if the responsibility for peopling Petalgeuse were hers. She covered everything from goat herding to proprequazincidental science and even had a few candidates in mind. "Give me a title, Queen Catherine will do, and I will populate the place."

"You can't be a queen," said Pinn. "Wrong sex, but you can be C.E.O. if you want."

"Are you saying you're a slut, sister?'"

Catherine sneered and went for another drink. At about that time, Nellie turned up holographically. She had been lying in bed reading Close Calls, by I.V., when her mind wandered. She knew Pinn would still be up. She had some questions about the meeting she too attended earlier. She thought it might be a quiet time to visit but was not surprised to find her daughters present.

"What's up," said Nellie's hologram, taking a seat to Pinn's left?

"Oh, hello mother," both girls replied in unison.

Catherine resumed her seat opposite Pinn. Michelle spoke.

"Pinn just made Catherine C.E.O. of the new world population and I am trying to convince him to relocate to Petalgeuse sooner rather than later."

The matriarch sat back and materialized a holographic cigarette, which produced holographic smoke after Pinn lit it.

"Petalgeuse did need to remain low key," she said exhaling, "but only the subterranean part needs to be kept secret. I imagine you will be living above ground for the time being. If you three are going, then so am I."

Michelle was chuffed. Catherine, not so much. Pinn was still not sure he was ready to go.

Six weeks later, early October 2027, the only three occupying the estate at Vevey, not counting a security team of six, a chef, two maids, three gardeners, and three drivers, were Justine and Izabella, almost eighteen, and Renée. All three girls said they had a few loose ends to tie up which they could not do from the never-never, but promised to be there by Christmas.

7.

On Pinn's second visit to Petalgeuse, a couple of years earlier, after a two and a half day validation session with the OyOyann, he excused himself and went outside for a cigarette. He ambled over to the pool where he was surprised to see Hermine casually lapping. She breast stroked, kept her head above water and piled her hair up on top of it to keep it dry.

"Join me," she invited as she approached Pinn who was leaning on the fence.

She took a mouthful of water and spurted it out in a steady arc for a stroke or two. Pinn smiled in declination. She stood, it was the shallow end of the pool, and waded in giant, swinging, slow-motion steps toward the edge. She was wearing a fluorescent pink bikini, but the color was not the attraction. Pinn could not pinpoint why she reminded him of someone.

"You have not changed a bit Pinn," Pinn heard from behind.

Turning, he faced an approaching Sugar, the same Sugar he knew twenty one years ago.

*

When Pinn questioned Bruce about how Sugar became mixed up in all this, he said it was a coincidence and spun the following yarn.

"After the couch toppled over all those years ago, instead of going back to your normal lives immediately as was supposed to happen, you two got held up in what we call the neithersphere for an extra forty five minutes, your time, where you continued to do what you were doing. When we picked up the error, we extracted you and put you back on track.

"Carelessly, we overlooked Sugar, and she became lost to the cosmos for a number of years. We like to blame the neithersphere. During those years, she gave birth to a daughter and learned the art of Ssenllew from a cosmic charlatan named Yelworc who was chained to a species of the notorious blue trees of Gal.1257.o.uch for a crime he said he didn't commit. According to the prisoner, the only way he could be freed was if he could convince some soul to trust him and to give that soul something morally useful in return for that trust."

It so happened, Shamash, higher up Bruce's family tree, was in the Gal. galaxy about then picking up exotica for his sister Inanna when an old guy waiting by the launch pad told him of a girl and her child being held captive on Gal.1257.o.uch. The old man said the child was the daughter of he, the man touted to rival Shamash himself, in the ages to come.

Shamash thought he'd fly by and have a look. He liked what he saw, and he took the woman and the child from the chained charlatan. The charlatan pleaded with Shamash not to take her. It had been ten years of hard work, he said, the woman was only one step away from affirming a state that would exonerate him and free him from the tree. Shamash didn't care.

Shamash was taken by the earthly female and she with him. Overnight she became his favorite consort. Inanna didn't like Sugar or the child and made their lives as uncomfortable for them as she could.

"Not long ago, Shamash sought to provide Sugar and Hermine with some respite from Inanna's harassment. He heard of the project I had going on, on the Orion-Cygnus arm of *via lactea* and he wondered if I had a place for the girls to rest and recreate.

"It was here the Wellness Retreat entered my mind.

"I explained to Shamash why I had an interest in the species on the planet, leaving out the part about the Tree of Life.

"Shamash told me what the old man told him. The child was the daughter of he, the man touted to rival Shamash himself in the ages to come.

"I saw no reason to deceive the greater power. As I heard it, I reported to Shamash, it will be Sumonus, the half brother of the girl, not the father who will ultimately vie for your authority.

"Before he nodded, releasing the girls to my care, Shamash cast me a frightening glare. It had knowing and warning.

"I was just as surprised as you to learn the woman was Sugar. Coincidence."

8.

Catherine had been trying to persuade Pinn to allow John John to visit Petalgeuse for some time, but Pinn kept putting her off. To compensate, she and Lilita, every so often, would take a week and visit John John in the Caymans or Anchorage or somewhere.

One day, both Minerva and Mia forecast possible deaths in the outcome of a trip Catherine was planning to take to Johannesburg nine days hence. Lilita would be with her and along with a male in his late thirties, possibly John John, all three would die.

Remembering how it felt to be suddenly Gormless, Pinn experienced trepidation.

According to the muses, a road accident was possible. It would be brought on by the haste of the driver of the open top coupe in which they all traveled. The vehicle would clip a pole at a corner and roll three times throwing its occupants, who were not wearing seat belts, willy-nilly into the air before coming to rest against a barbed-wired fence. "A number of seemingly unrelated incidents have to present in the right sequence for the event to occur," Miss Trust pointed out, "but it is there."

*

Pinn found Catherine on level seven of Petalgeuse proper talking to Garth.

Level seven contained the water processing plant. It had machinery and large tanks everywhere and was industrially noisy. Everything about the plant on this level was self-maintaining, Garth, an OyOyan, was yelling at Catherine, "A team of Embots (maintenance bots) patched this, tightened that, rewired the other and took care of themselves as well. Any mid-level gamer could handle the plant, but you would need an engineer, an electrician, and a fitter and turner if you had to go manual."

Nodding at Garth, Pinn put his arm through Catherine's arm and maneuvered her toward the elevators and a few less distressibles.

"You came all this way to see me Pinn," cooed Catherine as they walked, "how sweet. What can I do for you?"

While waiting for the elevator, Pinn established Catherine was going to Johannesburg as predicted, described the warnings the muses had reported, and suggested she not go.

"They don't let you out much do they Pinn," responded Catherine?

During the elevator ride back to New Cubus, husband and wife resolved Pinn's procrastination regarding John John visiting. One month after her return from Johannesburg, not going to Johannesburg was not negotiable, John John would be invited to stay for a week in the guest quarters inside the family compound at Petalgeuse. If all went well, the visits would continue. Catherine wanted John John to be among the final numbers when Petalgeuse closed off to the outside world.

*

Catherine and Lilita went to Johannesburg as planned and on the third day, along with John John, all three took a drive to see the Cradle of Humankind about 50 kilometers northwest of the city. John John had somehow procured a 1971 Stutz Black Hawk convertible in blood red with ivory (colored) trim for the jaunt. They traveled gaily to their destination. During the tour, John John received a call he said he had to take and twenty minutes later boarded a helicopter that set down on a small lawn to the left of the main entrance.

A driver disembarked from the helicopter as John John climbed aboard. His name was Allonzo, and he looked young. He was waiting by the car when the girls finished seeing John John off.

A small incident occurred as Allonzo chauffeured the girls back to their lodgings, but it would take a greater imagination than mine to turn it into a fatal event.

Too quickly, the month after Catherine's return from Johannesburg came around and John John arrived at Petalgeuse.

Pinn kept busy and out of the J's way but a couple of days before he was due to leave, during a dinner where all were present, John John told Pinn he hadn't been on a horse for years and asked if he and Pinn could take a ride together before he left. The day after next was good for him. Pinn was not keen but could not refuse.

Most days at Petalgeuse, start hot and get hotter. Fortunately, on this February morning the gods smiled upon the pair and produced a hazy low. The sun was there but greyed down by clouds that seemed to float behind it sometimes. A dry drizzle made it seem cooler.

Pinn reckoned they rode the two hours to the site with the odd rock formation where there would be refreshments awaiting them in comparative silence, but that was not the case. John John rabbited on the whole way. About ReadMe, about the weather, not the weather where they were, but globally, the inconvenience of war, Lilita, the Wellness Retreat, and more.

When Pinn finally tuned in, they were getting off their horses.

John John kept talking as they made their way to a table set out for them near the rock formation but changed the subject. He praised Pinn's extraordinary skill and good fortune when it came to managing his supply chain. "In the current climate," John John went on, "my numbers people put your company's performance in that area in the paranormal category."

A short distance from the table, he stopped and turned to face Pinn. "It's like all you had to do when you came to a closed door was say, 'open sesame,' and it opened."

The rock formation rumbled and split in two to reveal a cave and a tunnel.

Pinn went for a cheeseburger. He finished that and was eating a lime sorbet-coated vanilla ice cream on a stick, by the time John John closed his mouth and joined him.

Pinn uttered "emases nepo," and the rocks rumbled back into their original formation.

John John finished his bacon and egg roll, wiped his mouth and said, "open sesame."

The rocks rumbled open.

"Emases nepo," said Pinn.

The rocks rumbled shut.

After John John slurped the dregs of his chocolate milkshake, he was just about to say open sesame again when he was slugged by an electric shock of good current.

It was a condition for anybody visiting Petalgeuse for the first time to have the ReadMe IR27I9RM.B chip installed. The chip Snake and Stheno modified to facilitate the updated Voya.

When John John got up off the ground, a little froth and dribble around the left corner of his mouth, his humor had completely changed.

"There are two options," Pinn told John John while a burly caterer restrained him. "We can do the M.I.B. thing and remove the last fifteen minutes or whatever of your memory, change the command to the rock, just in case, and carry on as if all this never happened, or you can begin to live with Voya and perhaps be invited back."

9.

Pinn worked best if left to his own pace. It was generally slow with a hint of laziness. To the OyOyann, it appeared he was not keeping up. By late 2028, the list of critical issues relating to Petalgeuse's readiness to do battle was so long Bruce felt he had to intervene. It was less than fifteen months before Shamash would return to pick up Sugar, himself, and the rest of the OyOyann team.

Regardless of everything else, the major problem was the disgruntlement among Bruce's people about the lack of Earthlings to take over the tasks they were currently performing. According to Bruce, his people reckoned Pinn's people were acting like royalty, living a carefree existence above ground while in the underworld, the OyOyann toiled to power, water, feed, and service the illusion.

In response, Pinn said he could see what Bruce was getting at but suggested he was being a little harsh. Some of his people (Pinn's) were, indeed, working in the underworld alongside his people (Bruce's). And all people, from time to time, pursued recreational activities above ground and spent time among the family.

To ease the alien's angst, Pinn laid out where they were at in their readiness.

"Nearly all storage units were full. There were a few things missing but only one was critical. All utilities were humming along just nicely, livestock are healthy, and a cycle is being created. It is the same with the agricultural facility."

"All being done by my people," interrupted Bruce, "proving my point."

Pinn did not address Bruce's comment and went on.

"We are about to begin the selection process for the staff.

"Catherine has been getting to know the OyOyann operators and assessing their positions from their point of view as well as her own. From those meetings, she developed a profile for each position, which she forwarded to her assistants, Brittany and Smitten who then scoured numerous data bases and social media platforms for appropriate candidates. They narrowed the pool down to three hundred and sixty people for twenty-four positions."

"That still leaves six vacant berths," said Bruce.

Pinn nodded but did not get distracted from where he was going.

"Starting February one," he continued, "a few months from now, groups of thirty will arrive to begin a twenty-one-day wellness retreat where they will be assessed for the positions we need to fill. Your people have agreed to help select the most appropriate candidate for the discipline they serve. At the end of those three weeks, or just after, someone from each group will be given the role.

"We will start at the heart and work with power and utilities first, then move on to animal husbandry, agriculture, production, etc., all of which are at a sustainable operating status at this time, as you said, thanks to your people. It will take about eight and a half months to get through all the candidates, but when we do, we will be adequately manned. We should finish the process in about the middle of September, a full six weeks before the arrival of Shamash.

"Including contractors, come February, the average daily population at Petalgeuse will be eighty to ninety. Almost a third over R.P.N.—recommended passenger numbers."

"Grand plans," said Bruce. "Good luck. That still leaves six vacant berths."

*

For the three hundred and sixty candidates, winning one of the twenty-four positions was not easy. In the first week, they would be tested scholastically on how well they knew their jobs. The next week, while doing an above ground version of their job, their team spirit would be measured, and finally, in the last week, their ability to stay focused in the face of finality would be weighed.

It was envisioned that the analysis of the candidature for each position could, in some cases, result in a draw at the end of the twenty-one-day period. In that event, the rest would be sent back to from whence they came while the remaining few would have to face another three steps.

The three steps started with Dr. Glitch Hellicot. Dr. Glitch Hellicot was a noted psychiatrist famous for his work with ayahuasca and other hallucinogens. He developed a test not unlike Turing's AI test which went a step further and determined whether an intelligence had a soul.

The test involved answering questions and envisioning scenarios while a magnetic resonance imager monitored the subject's heart and brain activity. The patterning, as they went through the specifically tailored program was supposed to light up the brain in a zon^8 crystal formation as it and the heart synchronized.

Unfortunately, Dr. Hellicot did not detect anything that even vaguely resembled a soul using his methodology in his life time, but his approach did yield other key performance indicators that went to an individual's potential.

10.

To backtrack a little, Pinn first contacted Dr. Hellicot and invited him to Vevey after reading an article he wrote for the Désinvolte, a weekly magazine with a small circulation in the arrondissement du Montparnasse, Paris titled, Summanus (the God of distant thunder). Ramone came across the article one morning soon after it was issued and suggested Pinn read it. The piece outlined the problems closed loop societies generally face, and why, as experiments, they fail.

After Dr. Glitch caught Pinn's interest, Pinn delved into the life and times of the man through various publications and channels and learned about the soul determining machine and what it could discover, besides, even if it had not yet succeeded in its basic goal.

Face to face with the good doctor, Pinn asked why closed loop social experiments fail.

"Ignorance, innocence," he said. "The two words are interchangeable here. Both traits cannot be taught. They are genetic, but once corrupted, are gone forever.

"What most experiments are looking at creating," he continued, "is a nirvana, an ideal, a unity, a situation where individuals accept the whole above self-interest. Innocence or ignorance? It can't be done. Not now. Not this far past expulsion. You can't undo paradise lost."

A little evangelistic Pinn thought. Nevertheless, he persisted.

"Soon I will begin interviewing three hundred and sixty candidates for twenty-four positions in a closed loop social experiment I will be sponsoring over the next few years. I am disappointed you think such an experiment cannot succeed, but if it could, what profile would you project, Dr Glitch, for a successful candidate, and could we - you - test for it?"

After pondering a little, pacing and rubbing his chin, he said, "Starting with the basics, to create self-perpetuance in a module in terms of the psyche of the inhabitants, you must sacrifice people of greed, lust, and covertness for youth, health and hope."

Suspicious Pinn asked Dr. Hellicot to which religion he ascribed. None, he answered. A religious discussion between the two followed. It was long and sometimes deep but a truly tiresome read so we will skip it.

Three hours later they came up with this: The perfect candidates for the Petalgeuse experiment should be between the ages of sixteen and twenty-seven, be of sound health, have modest habits, and a gender that equals their genitalia.

Ninety percent of Catherine's three hundred and sixty candidates fit the age group. Pinn was happy.

11.

Notwithstanding the H.R. issues, Petalgeuse was motoring along well by autumn. Frank was at the helm. Things were getting done and everybody was settling in.

Since moving to Petalgeuse, Pinn found he wanted to spend less time in an office environment and more time getting in touch. Whatever that meant. He was always wired, so to speak, so he was not uncontactable if he was out unless he wanted to be. In the mornings he wandered the grounds and sat, and watched, and pondered, sometimes accompanied, mostly alone. In the evenings, often until late, he wandered through the underground. Gene took to joining Pinn for his underground jaunts. He, the dog, liked to promote his status to whomever they came across, whether beast or being.

Early one morning, around six am, Pinn was walking alone when he came across Sugar bathing in a small billabong a few hundred meters east of the compound. It was the only place on the whole lease where bushes and trees grew with any confidence. It was close to where the dry rivers met and shielded from the compound by its foliage. When Pinn first discovered the little oasis, he had a bench with a back installed. He used the site often but had never swum in its waters.

She was sitting on a rock, in profile, half a thigh deep in the clear pool, scooping water over her naked self with a cupped right hand. With each scoop, she leaned back slightly. A white robe hung on a snapped branch close by.

Pinn considered fleeing. But the wellness mother sensed all and suspected he might. She stood and turned to face him. She wished him a good morning with an angelic smile and a slight slackening of her left knee.

She could see Pinn's pleasure grow at the surprise encounter but received no reply.

"Sit," she said after a while. He did. On the bench. He watched as she fetched her robe and joined him. She still smelled of pink fairy floss.

"Would you like me to fix that," she asked, sidling up to Pinn.

She was joking, she wiggled in fun, then sidled away. But she kept up the distraction during the conversation. Now and again a breast or both would pop out of her robe to say hello as she gesticulated through some description or made a point. Casually and caressingly, she would pop them back undercover when she noticed and pretend to adjust her sash.

At first, they talked about Shamash. It was August, two months before Shamash's return.

Pinn feared Shamash. He, Shamash had been told that he, Pinn would usurp him. Pinn didn't feel much like a usurper and suspected Bruce was right about the usurper being his son, which only increased his dread.

"But," he said, "if it were only myself to consider, I would gladly face the wrath of the majesty of all phalli for the touch of your fingertips one more time."

"So that's a yes then," questioned Sugar?

Seconds later, her demeanor changed. She stood, tucked everything in, and tightened her sash. She began to amble to and fro in front of Pinn. Each leg of her toing and froing was four, five, or six paces in length and formed the parabola of her concern. Halfway through the sixth fro, she stopped in front of Pinn and turned to face him. For a full minute, she just stared at him with big eyes. Once or twice, it looked like she might say something, but she didn't. She gave up. She resumed her pacing briefly before returning to her seat on the bench.

She spoke about her abandonment, the anguish of not being able to return to her children, the twilight into which Hermine was born, and the years spent with Yelworc. It was not just the length of his chain that needed to be measured, she said.

In the beginning, she was alone, desperate, and in need but as time passed the situation improved. Hermine grew to be a sprightly young lass and then Shamash turned up.

It was quite the change for Hermine, and herself too, suddenly living in the realms of the next level super-rich whose everything is all there is.

Initially, Hermine was impressed but soon realized she was not considered one of them. Inanna was exceptionally good at reminding her. It affected Hermine badly at first, she was eleven. One day, something happened on the way to the forum. She did not tell her mother exactly what occurred but said it involved an older Neph and a small hole in a wall, adding, a point was proved.

"After that, Hermine settled down, went about her business, took what she could in, and kept out of the way. She seemed happy enough, and then Shamash, God bless his soul, sent us here. Since then, Hermine has blossomed, and we have both had something to do."

"George would have been proud," said Pinn.

"Proud of what," asked Sugar? "George is not Hermine's father, you are."

Pinn responded with disbelief. He didn't think they mated on that night all those years ago.

Sugar described the moments after they fell into the neithersphere in such detail that Pinn conceded it happened.

"I thought it was a dream," said Pinn

"It was," said Sugar, "but we are here now."

Sugar thought the relationship between himself and Hermine a little too flirty for a father and a daughter, especially in the current, narrow, environment.

"She started it," said Pinn. "I didn't know who she was."

"But now that you do know, you will be the adult, right?"

Pin asked if Hermine knew he was her father? Sugar replied, "Yes, I told her the night we arrived at Petalgeuse."

A discussion followed that wavered in intensity. Pinn stood and paced. The rendezvous ended when they said at the same time, surprising each other, "only if she wants to become one of them."

12.

It was not the Love Boat, but Izabella thought Petalgeuse should have a social calendar. From when the first candidates started to arrive for assessment, she began organizing BBQs, games nights, movie nights, karaoke, that sort of thing, with Frank and Sugar's blessing and support. By the middle of September, when all positions were filled, she wanted to celebrate with a party and invite outsiders. She thought Halloween might be nice.

She went to her father who was expecting her. He had assembled a quorum. They were having a stand-up breakfast of fruits, quiche, muffins, and coffee down by the pool. Bruce, Ramone, Snake, the Grubb, Dip, Frank, Sugar, Jacob, and Michelle were present. Catherine was in Dublin with Lilita. Renee was conducting a calisthenics class for the new recruits and the youngen's, the boys, Sumonus and Atlaseze, across the way near the tennis courts.

After selecting a muffin, Izabella presented her case for holding a Halloween party where outside guests could be invited that displayed a fairly in-depth knowledge of the state of the ark.

There was a barrage of objections in the beginning which Izabella let wash over her, but as things progressed and concessions were made where concessions could be made, the bottom line for all was that there seemed something smug about inviting guests to a lavish party at a secret haven before expelling them from it at the midnight hour.

"It will be before midnight," said Izabella.

"It's easier to keep folks out than throw them out," said Jacob.

Izabella was beginning to be swayed by Jacob. Zac, the young OyOyann, was not happy. She spent more time with him than he at the functions she organized he complained. At a karaoke night, where he butchered, "Raindrops Keep Falling on My Head," after stumbling off the stage, he suggested to her that Jacob had eyes for Hermine.

The big deal for Bruce was Shamash would be present and he was worried due respect could be wanting.

"He is traveling to reunite with his favorite consort," said Izabella. "It is an unofficial visit; let him relax."

"He arrives at the Hallowed eve's noon."

"Yes, and leaves at 9 pm Halloween. I am counting on that to get people out when the time comes. After watching the spectacle of Shamash's rocket launching to wherever with you lot on board, three hours later, or just before midnight when Petalgeuse goes into stage one lockdown, we replicate the event with a dummy rocket which will take all guests to Sydney where appropriate connecting transport will be waiting.

"That still doesn't address motive," said Michelle. "Who are we inviting and why?"

"For some of us," Izabella answered, "there are people we would like to see one more time, for others, aware of the berth's still available, there are people they think are suitable to fill them. I know mother would like to see John John selected.

"You wouldn't want Lilita to grow up without her father now, would you daddy," said Izabella?

"It would suit me fine," muttered Pinn.

*

The quorum voted against the party by a considerable margin, the boys v the girls essentially, but Pinn overturned the result. He felt a Halloween party would keep everybody focused and busy, especially since it would be the day of stage one lockdown.

Guests from the outside world, however, could not be invited. Izabella was miffed and it took some time before she could be placated. But she soon came up with a plan B and all was well.

Meanwhile, Pinn was trying to get a shipment of a hundred and eighty liters of hydrargyrum from the reservoir beneath the temple of the Feathered Serpent delivered. That quantity of the element from that site, due to its prior use, would produce at least six hundred stiles of exquanomaltine, enough to tip the dawn of the new yuga. The OyOyann insisted it should be sought and stored. Bruce had built a special facility for it at true north on the west wall of level one.

An old Ord, who was a hundred and three and unwell from first contact, was supposed to supply it but died a few days after the contract was signed. Supposedly, no one else knew how to get to the purported reservoir beneath the sacred site.

Pinn had been dithering with the problem when one night he mentioned it to Catherine who mentioned it to John John, who reckoned it couldn't be true. Someone must know how to get to the reservoir below the temple. After making a few calls he learned that a girlfriend of Castel's uncle's sister's daughter, his contact in Mexico, knew the brother of a laborer's son who worked with the old Ord at one time and says he knows the way to the reservoir.

What are the odds?

John John offered to go to Mexico and arrange the shipment.

Again, Pinn could not refuse his offer.

"Considering the social climate and the weather out there it could be quite dangerous," Pinn pointed out.

"No shit," said Catherine, butting in, "Much of America's south is experiencing an extreme weather event they are calling la madre del diablo

There are floods, landslides, enormous infrastructure damage, outages, and deaths. If they let you onto the continent, it's practically impossible to get anything or to move anywhere, especially around Mexico. Quetzalcoatl may be rubble or underwater."

John John said he could handle it. Catherine said she was going with him. Pinn said okay.

Catherine and John John dropped Lilita off at Petalgeuse on their way to Mexico City and said they'd be back by Halloween.

13.

There must have been something in the air. Bruce rarely spoke so frankly and almost always avoided long term detail. But during this October discussion he was uncharacteristically enlightening.

They were at the usual table by the pool. One had coffee, one had tea, one smoked and no one swam. The morning was a cool twenty-four degrees Celsius.

"Tell me again why you want to save us," said Pinn?

"I didn't say I wanted to save you," said Bruce, "I said I wanted to save the planet."

"Arguable. In your Shamash story, you also mentioned the Tree of Life. What's the Tree of Life got to do with anything? I thought I signed on to captain a ship to a settlement in a new world, not join a quest to find the Tree of Life."

"You did and you didn't. It's not lost, the tree," said Bruce, "and therein lies the opportunity."

"For you or for me?"

"For us both."

Bruce stood and walked to a mesh fence that stopped one from falling into the desert. Its top rail was high enough for him to rest his clasped arms upon. He looked out onto the vastness. Pinn swiveled his seat to face him.

Taking an unfamiliar tone Bruce talked through the early years of his life, the joy of boyhood, the anxiety of youth, the relationship with his younger brother, and the anger he felt when he learned his younger brother held seniority by the law of the seed.

To Bruce, it seemed his father didn't like him. He sent him off as a cadet to Ea when he was young. Ten thousand years later he was recalled by his father and instructed to survey planet Earth for anatomic gold. He was given a small team.

Without his brother or his father, Bruce became lord of the Earth. He found significant deposits of the mineral his father sought but needed miners to extract it. He reported there was a species of hominid on the planet, but their development was hundreds of thousands of years behind what was useful. Their needs were basic and their means of fulfilling them were simple. They were erect, had opposable thumbs, and were easily subjugated.

Bruce's brother, his entourage, and two thousand working hands turned up a short time later. The two brothers couldn't work together, so their father was called. He divided the world into three segments. To Bruce, he allotted the underworld, the southern hemisphere, where the gold was mined, and half the workers. To his brother he allotted the upper world, the northern hemisphere where a sustainable city or two should be built, and to himself, to watch over all, he allotted the skies above, the heavens.

The big guy drew a big sigh then phrased it before choosing words and continuing.

"Many years had gone by since Ninhursag and I began engineering the hominid. The time came when we had to trust the being we had created and plug it into the power. The allegory with the apple is cute but the actual journey to that point was tough.

"People have pondered the Garden of Eden story for thousands of years – Adam, Eve, the talking snake, the Tree of Life, the Tree of Knowledge, the apple. Some may have even asked why the Tree of Life was a non-player back then but has been all the rage ever since.

"I was there, I was the so-called, snake," said Bruce. "Let me tell you, briefly, how the day unfolded.

"Possibly the most relatable description of Adam and Eve, as they were represented in Eden, is as hippies living a naked and care free life in a paradise with no responsibilities. Not even to each other. But nothing could have been further from the truth. They were created to be an encumbered race, which I fostered, and my brother embraced.

"At creation, it was deemed that Adam and Eve would be affected by time, not sin as popularly understood.

"It meant Adam and Eve would transition through certain levels of growth, procreate, age, and then perish.

"Perish was the word that saved me at council.

"It was a weekend, a Saturday morning. I found Adam down by the brook, sitting naked on a rock. His feet were in the water, and he leaned forward to clasp his hands around his knees. He rocked on the rock slightly and he was trying to vocalize a tune. He was about eighteen.

"The language we spoke then was somewhat different to that which we speak now, but translated and condensed, my encounters went as follows.

"I stepped up the pressure. I had suggested to Adam some months back that maybe there was something better in life than eating melons, playing with his navel, and thinking with his dick.

"We can change the first two," I told him. "You can discover better ways to spend your time. But we cannot change the third."

"That would have been all right with Adam except Adam was a creature of habit. He could not do without his melons and berries with a squeeze of honey in the morning, and it didn't matter to him that he would not learn how to cultivate, hunt, build, explore, covet, question, confront, abuse, smoke, understand, drink, invent, conquer, or fish. He was happy enough in Eden where everything was laid on for him. All he wanted was to have a conversation with the young gazelle who timidly appeared at the water's edge opposite during my visit.

"Later I came across Eve in the midst of the garden, twirling, head thrown back, arms outstretched, giggling. Shortly, giddiness overcame her and she collapsed onto a lush bed of soft moss by a scarlet bush with silver buds.

"I offered her my hand to help her up. Eve was happy to see me and gladly accepted. As she reached her feet, she saw desire in my eyes and pulled my hand to her breasts.

"I am not known for my fidelity but did not proceed on this occasion. The words of Nintu rang in my head – enness unnui de fai sin trizt san u tzir. I removed my hand.

"We were mere meters from the Tree of Knowledge. I led the slightly grubby and naked Eve toward it.

"It was much easier to impress Eve with promises of learning what the gods know and inheriting that power on Earth than it was to interest Adam. It was around lunchtime. Eve was hungry and the fruit of the tree looked plump, pink, and delicious.

"I told her wondrousness's would never cease and that she would become the mother of all if she were to show Adam what to do with the fruit of the tree."

"It's forbidden," she said.

"It is," I responded.

"To our left bloomed the Tree of Life.

"Adam approached; I went behind a bush.

"Adam had come to tell Eve about the cheeky gazelle he had met by the creek earlier but Eve was not interested. She asked Adam if he was hungry. He told her he was hungry enough to eat two melons. Eve told Adam as she reached up with both hands that they did not have melons, but they had these…. She plucked a fruit from the Tree of Knowledge. It's forbidden, said Adam. Yes, twinkled Eve, taking a bite of the fruit, then holding it toward Adam so he could too.

"The instant Adam took a bite, a flaming sword appeared before the Tree of Life, and I was summoned to council.

"Between you and I," concluded Bruce, "on that day, I was the proudest dad on Earth."

"Might be why you have a reputation as a devil," said Pinn.

*

Bruce believed the Tree of Life would have lesser value if knowledge was not acquired first. His plan had always been to guide an eligible candidate to it when the time was right. It had taken him a Noah and countless other catastrophes but finally, things looked like they might align. Bruce began to think his ambition to engineer an immortal from a hominid was achievable.

The immortals, Shamash's circle, did not welcome new arrivals. It meant battle. Most who heard of such a threat quashed it outright.

"I don't want to become an immortal," said Pinn.

"You won't," answered Bruce, "but you are the father of he who could, so it's important we do not speak of it, or it is not spoken about by anyone for the duration of Shamash's upcoming visit."

"But he knows; you told him yourself," said Pinn. "Your exact words; 'As I heard it, it will be Sumonus, the half-brother of the girl, not the father who will ultimately vie for your authority'."

"Protocol," said Bruce. "Covering myself. I am sure Shamash hasn't spoken about it since, and I expect he will

185

expect you haven't either. There should be no problem unless he has already decided to have you killed. For reasons to be revealed later, it's unlikely he has made that decision yet, so relax."

"Comforting," said Pinn."

"When Shamash is in town, three weeks from now, my advice is this; you are no physical match for him Pinn. Unfortunately, there is an irritating elitism in your rhetoric that can be irksome if not successful as humor. So be careful. You cannot avoid Shamash. He would be insulted, and it would give him a reason to have you dispatched. Keep Michelle with you at all times. He will have Sugar with him. And keep your mouth shut; let the women talk. Shamash has no humor but a lot of might, remember that. He could smite you there and then if one of your off the cuff remarks offends him."

"Smite?"

"Yes."

14.

During its perigee period in March 2029, Venus came closer to the planet than it had for more than six thousand years. The Earth showed its displeasure at the bullish behavior with an increase in earthquake activity, volcanic eruptions, and destructive storms.

A few months later as she moved off for a time the weather and seismic activity eased. Folks thought the worst was over.

*

Sitting around the breakfast table on Halloween eve, Pinn wondered out loud how they were going to land a sizeable rocket secretly at Petalgeuse through all this clear weather, and then launch it again the following evening, again, secretly.

"Time minusculisation," said Sugar, buttering fruit toast. "The opposite of time aeternus. These guys know how to use both. You will enjoy the show; it's impressive."

The boys, fourteen, between mouthfuls of toasted muesli with dried fruits, nuts, milk, and sugar, expressed an interest in seeing both the landing and the launch, as did most present - Michelle, Renée, Hermine, Justine, Izabella, Lilita, Gustaf and Greta. Catherine and John John had left Mexico City a day ago and were expected to arrive back at Petalgeuse three hours after Shamash.

"Viewing the movements of Shamash's rocket shouldn't be a problem," said Pinn, "but," he continued, "we should review our strategy, as a family, for the next two days while we are all together."

"Too busy," said Izabella, standing, gulping down the last of her coffee. "Got a reception, a BBQ, and a party to organize." She continued to hold a triangle of marmalade toast. "Nobody is to talk about Sumonus," she caricatured, "and he is to be kept out of sight. Got it." She raised her spare hand to the side of her mouth, pinched her thumb and forefinger, and made as if to zip it before turning and disappearing out a door.

Hermine excused herself also and left. She offered no excuse and while her mother was not happy with that, Pinn had no qualms.

The boys were disgruntled. Atlaseze particularly. His argument was it was unfair to restrict him just because his brother supposedly exists in some futuristic science fiction fantasy.

Renee, sitting between her son and Lilita, comforted him and refilled his juice.

"Shamash will be staying in the west wing," said Pinn. "The rooves are high enough there. But he will be in public spaces from time to time from early in the afternoon today until just before twenty one hundred hours tomorrow."

He told the boys they could watch the landing from the balcony of the west wing with everybody else. But immediately after the engines of the rocket were shut down, they were to return to the compound and their underground quarters and remain there until Shamash's departure. At his departure, they will be escorted back to the west wing to witness the lift off by Gustaf and Greta who will be their chaperones for the duration."

Lilita left; said she was going to help Izabella.

"Tomorrow is Halloween, father," said Sumonus.

"Correct."

"And there is to be a Halloween party."

"Two out of two," said Pinn.

"Since most at such a party are either costumed or disguised, why could we not attend if we were adequately masked," asked Sumonus?

"Because everybody would still know who you are," said Sugar, "regardless of outfitting, and it would not take long until Shamash did too."

Michelle was about to interject but a look from Sumonus and a slight gesture indicated to his mother that all was well.

Sumonus continued; "With all due respect, Wellness Mother, it is unlikely Shamash has given me any thought at all. He is coming to collect his favorite consort and I expect his mind will be on other things."

"That might be," said Sugar. "I have seen it cross your mind. But, under the circumstances, you are mistaken if you think that that is the reason he is coming. Any one of his people could have picked us up and he is never short of company if he so desires. He wants to see he who is to challenge him. And judging by your attitude, young man, you sound like you want to do it today. He is a Goliath, Sumonus; you are no David."

"Nice touch," said Michelle.

"I am not afraid mother," said Sumonus.

"I am," said Pinn interrupting. "I have no desire to be smote just yet."

Pinn let himself be persuaded to ease Atlaseze and Sumonus's restrictions. They could still watch Shamash's arrival and departure from the west wing balcony with everybody else, but now they could also attend the Halloween party between the hours of six and eight and join in the games and other festivities as long as Sumonus was costumed to include a side kick, like the Lone Ranger and Tonto. Someone to stay close to him throughout the proceedings.

*

After breakfast, Pinn set out on horseback to the site where Shamash would land and launch his rocket. The facility lay to the north, northwest three kilometers beyond the stables. It popped up out of the ground earlier that morning thanks to the astonishing engineering of the site. When it was no longer needed it would drop back into the slab.

About half a kilometer out from his destination, Pinn noticed Bruce standing alone in the desert by a clump of tall xanthorrhoea, gazing northward.

Pinn dismounted and walked toward Bruce.

"Admiring your handiwork," asked Pinn as he approached?

Bruce turned and then turned back.

"Immortality, according to the epic poem," he said, "is achieved through the worth of one's work. A brick wall if that is your occupation. After that, it is recommended you hold your children's hand, hope you give them enough courage to do the same with their children, and in the end, accept fate. Death everlasting. A bit of a letdown after all that adventure don't you think?"

"Everlasting death, when the time comes, sounds like a blessing to me," said Pinn.

"The poem, like all poems, encrypts its knowledge and in doing so becomes entangled in its own whimsical relationship with it and ends up presenting a closed loop that is touted as something else but still offers no escape.

"Breaking the loop is not so hard," said Bruce.

"Not for a god maybe," said Pinn.

"With care, you could become, sorry, not you, your son Sumonus, could become an actual immortal, not an honorary one like Utnapishtim. A player. But you have to survive the catastrophe first."

"Why pick me," asked Pinn? "There were others. Many others. I was just doing what I did every day at that time. Sit on an empty bench overlooking the beach. Harming no one. But then you turn up and I am dragged into a journey that brings me to here, now. Not trying to save all of humanity, but a select few."

"On an earthly scale perhaps," said Bruce, "but universally you are trying to save an endangered species."

*

On his return to the compound, Pinn came across Izabella six rungs up a ladder stringing lights.

"Looking good," said Pinn.

"You need to talk to Snake," she said. "He is giving me grief about our power consumption. Said something about how much is being diverted for Shamash's needs."

"I will," said Pinn continuing on his way.

He came across Frank and Jacob before he reached the elevator to the underworld where he was headed. New Cubus specifically.

Frank spoke about how he missed Sugar already. Usually, it was he and she who hosted the Petalgeuse parties but on the morrow, she was one of the honored guests.

Pinn asked him about the state of the ark to which Frank replied, "All hulls were full except the one awaiting the exquanomaltine but that was due in about five hours. There are thirteen non-residents on-site, four of which will drive out this afternoon; the other nine, caterers and entertainers, will depart on the second rocket tomorrow after the party. There is a little stress amongst personnel because tomorrow morning, for the first time, they will have to manage the environment themselves. The OyOyann assistance program terminates at dawn.

Summarizing Frank said, "So far so good."

Pinn looked at Jacob, who returned his gaze but said nothing.

*

"The tilt of the Earth has shifted since Venus's flyby earlier this year," said Snake, as Pinn entered New Cubus.

"Does that mean Shamash is going to touch down in the south paddock instead of at the landing site as expected,' asked Pinn?

"I don't know," said Snake, "but it has its concerns in terms of how little it took in the first pass to affect Earth and what is to come. Bruce knew all along, but it has taken us time to collate the data. Next time around, Venus will exert greater interference, more tilt maybe, a change in rotational velocity perhaps, then, less than a year later, osculation. We need to buckle up and hope these people knew what they were doing when they built this thing."

"The scammers?"

"Yes."

"We do," agreed Pinn, "but not until we get past Halloween."

"Really?"

"Yes. Tomorrow morning we will flick the facility onto auto pilot. It will be alright. I can't see the OyOyann leaving the place in a state that would cause them embarrassment during their exalted's stay. Later maybe, but not during. We go manual the instant Shamash leaves and make lock down."

Snake and the Grubb said they needed to be at their posts. They would be in the first hours of complete control of Petalgeuse. Pinn argued that that was precisely why auto pilot was suitable. The animals would be fed, the plants would be watered, the turbines would turn. "There are thirty three hours from Shamash's arrival to his departure, but we would only be on auto pilot for sixteen of them. What could go wrong?

"Later today there will be a reception followed by an informal BBQ in honor of our guest, he who provides the roof over our heads. It is imperative you attend. The pigs are already turning on spits. A Halloween come farewell party will follow tomorrow night. From his arrival to his departure you will need to remain available. You will be busy."

Pinn started toward his space on the other side of the room and was surprised to see Hermine lounging on a couch there. It reminded him of something, and he turned back.

"Izabella tells me you are restricting her power," Pinn directed to Snake.

"Not me," said Snake. "The launchpad is drawing most of our power and we are powerless to do anything about it."

"You told Izabella that."

"Yes."

"And she said?"

"I'm going to tell daddy on you."

Pinn returned his attention to Hermine.

Hermine swiveled from a lying down position to an upright sitting position as Pinn found his seat.

"What's up," he asked?

"I don't want to leave tomorrow," she said.

"Have you spoken to your mother?"

"No."

She got up and wandered over to a table near her father and leaned against it, arms and legs crossed.

"Why," asked Pinn?

"I'm not one of them," she said.

She spoke about Inanna's complete hatred of her, Shamash's indifference, and other folks' veiled delusions of superiority just because they were a little taller and lived a little longer. Here, on Earth, she felt she could engage in the life she was meant to pursue and on equal footing.

"I meant why haven't you spoken to your mother."

When he received no answer, Pinn went on.

"So, what's the plan,' he asked?

"None. That's why I came to you. I hoped you would want me to stay too."

"She will think you have seduced me," said Pinn.

"No, she will think you have seduced me," said Hermine.

It was decided they would not tell Sugar of her daughters' desire to stay and would work out a way for her to miss the launch.

15.

Except for the landing, which was every bit as spectacular as Sugar implied it could be, Shamash's arrival turned out to be a non-event. His shuttle from the rocket took him straight to his accommodations bypassing the planned reception. Thirty minutes later, he appeared on the west wing balcony. He scanned the surrounds and the facility for a few minutes before disappearing back inside.

"He looks tall," said Pinn.

"Nine feet, they say," said Frank.

*

Hermine was at the landing site with her mother when Shamash came down. She said he looked cranky, pushed past Bruce, barely acknowledged mother, and yelled something at the shuttle pilot before hitting his head climbing into it. They traveled in silence to the west wing. Once there, Shamash began to cool. The rooves of the west wing were high enough and he didn't have to stoop or duck to move between rooms. There were flagons of wine, Gnangara Shiraz from the 1980's, wheels of King Island Brie and loaves of crusty soft bread. The OyOyann carpenter stationed at Petalgeuse had fashioned a magnificent day bed to Shamash's dimensions in his spare time especially for this visit. Once Shamash relaxed upon it some of us were free to go about our business."

"Will we see him at the BBQ tonight," asked Pinn?

"Yes, he is here to see Sumonus, and he will expect him to be there."

"He won't be."

"That's between you and him," said Hermine, "but be careful, you are dealing with a king. A king of great power. The only reason he hasn't done anything so far about this portended threat to his status is because he is expecting the cataclysm to wipe you all out, saving him the trouble of doing it."

"Yet you wish to stay."

"I would rather die in heaven than survive in hell."

*

There is no way of adequately describing the presence of Shamash. The earth quaked beneath his step, the heavens withdrew to give him room to stand upright, his erect hat added three feet to his height, and he commanded an aura that extended well beyond his mass.

His muscular arms were banded with gold, as was his waist and the flange of his headpiece. On one wrist he wore a petaled watch. His robes were haute couture in exquisitely woven, defensive by design, fabrics. His grooming, including a beard squared, was equally obsessive. On arrival, he carried a plain clutch bag in one hand and what looked like a large pinecone in the other, both of which he passed to an attendant shortly after arrival.

Shamash showed little interest in the Earthlings attending the BBQ at first. He was hungry and he had been smelling the spitting pigs for a good part of his stay on the planet.

Everybody ate and drank heartily, the OyOyann on one side of the courtyard, the Earthlings on the other.

You could hear Shamash's voice and laughter above the others sometimes, but nothing the OyOyann were saying could be understood. They spoke their own language.

On their side of the courtyard, Nellie and Michelle were catching up with Catherine and John John. They had returned to Petalgeuse earlier that day as expected and were still excited about their Mexican adventure. Izabella was describing to Justine, Renée, Lilita, Brittany, and Smitten how they would make the courtyard look tomorrow night for the Halloween party, and Frank, Pinn, Snake, the Grubb, Dip, Stheno, and Jacob were discussing generalities. They were relaxed.

Suddenly, the giant stood and strode to the Earthling end of the courtyard. He had been sitting on a chair his people brought with them. A throne. Six of his people picked it up by special grips at its base and followed Shamash to his new location where they set it down.

Shamash had been in many similar situations and found it was much easier to communicate meaningfully with lesser beings if he were seated and his face could be addressed more comfortably than his groin.

Everybody fell silent as he sat. He waved a hand and the noise level returned.

Just when things were settling down, there came an explosion of wind from between two legs that was loud, long, and rank.

Silence, fell again.

Some folks were impressed, others had to stop themselves from gagging.

When the air cleared, Shamash said, still seated, nobody wanted to see him stand, "let's get down to formalities."

Izabella took that as her cue and approached his mightiness. She welcomed him to the planet on behalf of Bruce, Pinn, and everybody present and praised his majesty for both his deeds and his godliness. She would have gone on but two of the throne bearers linked their arms through hers and marched her back to her seat, backwards.

"Where's Pinn," Shamash asked?

Pinn stood and said, "When we discussed your arrival, Bruce was afraid we would not provide the pomp and ceremony worthy of a figure of your stature. We tried but so far, it has been ignored. What do you want?"

"To meet your son, Sumonus," said Shamash.

"He's not here."

"Then get him"

"Forgive me sir," said Pinn, "but I am the captain of this ship."

"By my grace."

"Yes, thank you, and as such, what occurs and what does not occur on this vessel is up to my discretion."

Shamash leaned back on his throne, shoved a cushion above his buttocks and stretched his legs. His man refilled his drink. Sugar approached and whispered something in his ear. He smiled and shooed her away with a playful pinkie wave.

"It is your ship only in as much as you can defend it," said Shamash. Pinn heard Jacob breathe in.

Pinn lit a cigarette. The great man wanted one too. Human sized cigarettes were too small. There was a short wait while some XXXL Ramon's Allones, which Catherine and John John picked up on their Mexican trip in case such an occasion arose, were retrieved. At the same time, a tall, small table and a stool were brought in for Pinn.

Lit up and relaxed, Shamash crossed his legs and blew smoke rings.

"Why do you believe in the story," asked Pinn? "It's not written and the potenders' don't seem to be beacons of enlightenment to me. Who came up with the prediction in the first place?"

"Astrologer Lux."

"And he is?"

"Another honorary immortal like Utnapishtim, living on Skeral, in the loxin galaxy. He has a gift."

"I'm sure, said Pinn. "But, how does he get the detail, how do the constellations spell out, 'Sumonus, the stepbrother of the girl, for example?"

Shamash sat up and extended a flat, upright, open palm toward Bruce which meant he may not speak.

"We all know about Bruce's ambition," said Shamash. "We know the great lengths he has gone to, to get it to where it is, and we are aware conditions are beginning to favor an unauthorized success."

"My only interest is getting this boat from one port to another," said Pinn.

"And you are the father of he, Bruce expects to elevate," said Shamash. "The man who is going to save humankind, will, if successful, bring my foe of the future with him instead of him perishing, as he, et al, would have, had Bruce not intervened."

"You should take that up with Bruce," said Pinn.

Shamash leaned back again, slung one leg over the arm of his throne, and blew more smoke rings.

"It's a story," said Pinn.

"What?"

"The prediction, the prophecy."

"Oh, the Earth is not heading for a catastrophe?"

"It is," said Pinn. "I acknowledge that part. But for any speculator to speculate realistically on anything after the collision, they would need a collider and a particle science background."

"Or a crystal ball. You are right Earthling," said Shamash. "It all depends on who survives the cleansing. Patience is not one of my virtues. I apologize. I wish you well."

"But you hope we all burn, get crushed or drown."

"I do. Nonetheless," he said sitting upright, "I still want to meet the little Prïck they say will usurp me."

Pinn stood, bowed slightly in the direction of Shamash, and said before excusing himself and withdrawing, "Sumonus will be present at tomorrow night's celebrations for two hours."

"I look forward to it," Shamash said to Pinn's back.

16.

Most woke early on the morn of Halloween 2029. There was much to do. It was a good thing Petalgeuse was on auto pilot.

After a casual breakfast in the southern courtyard, where family and friends milled in groups, eating pancakes and maple bacon, sipping or quaffing cups of milk, tea, or juice, Pinn, Snake, the Grubb, Stheno, Frank, and Michelle descended into New Cubus.

"What's up," asked the Grubb when they arrived?

Pinn wanted to know if they were being surveilled by Shamash. Could Shamash see them now and hear what they were talking about?

Snake told him it was possible but unlikely. He said as Shamash's rocket was touching down, they detected the transmission of a sub decibel frequency with a link affix that they believed was preventing them from tapping into Shamash's communications. When the rocket landed, and the power was killed the transmission stopped and they were then able to hear the hum of standby activity in the vehicle and observe the vacant stations they couldn't before.

"Thinking that that would be the way to protect ourselves against spying from the aliens we managed to replicate the frequency and Grubb was able to create a unique link affix which changes every thirty minutes. We started transmitting shortly after Shamash arrived at the west wing and as far as we can tell, it works."

"What's up," Grubb asked again?

"Hermine does not want to leave the planet with her mother, and Shamash wants to meet Sumonus."

Everybody knew the second piece of information but not the first.

Pinn said he was afraid Shamash would take the opportunity to harm Sumonus.

Pinn instructed everybody to draw their chairs in and form a circle. When they were sitting knee to knee, Pinn bid all to lean forward until their heads touched and put an arm around each person beside them. They formed a human dome.

Inside the dome, in a low voice, Pinn explained their position and laid out a plan he thought would thwart Shamash.

It took about thirty minutes. Every now and then the dome had to dismantle so it could get some fresh air, stretch, and collect its thoughts. In the end, except where Hermine would miss the rocket, it wasn't really discussed, those present agreed on a course of action.

*

Sumonus decided to go to the Halloween party as the Batman. He spoke to Justine, his older sister about it and asked if she would be his Robin.

"The same uniform would be fine," he said, "as long as it's updated and fits. Just wear a short pleated mini skirt over the undies.

"Anything else," she asked?

"To do with this," said Sumonus, "no."

She smiled and agreed. She was fond of her younger brother.

Atlaseze was going as the Hulk, and Lilita as Lilita Goth.

Michelle visited the children in their rooms after the meeting and spent some time with them as they designed and printed their costumes. There was great excitement. Michelle suggested the boys bolster their costuming and give themselves a little extra height and brawn. The boys liked that idea. Makeup was all that was left to apply when it came time to don their masterpieces.

*

After lunch, Hermine was able to excuse herself from the west wing. She told her mother she had not completed packing up her rooms at Petalgeuse and she would be back before dusk. As she entered the main courtyard Stheno fell into step beside her. "Pinn is waiting for you at the billabong," she said.

Hermine was not sure where she meant so Stheno escorted her to the southern perimeter of the compound and directed her to follow the barely discernible track between the two more obvious ones.

Pinn and Hermine spent a relatively short time together at the billabong. Pinn said he was still working on a plan where she would miss the launch. Meanwhile, she should do what she is expected to do.

"If I can't get back to you," he said, "someone else will."

Hermine was not happy. She was half made up for the party. Her hair was as it was the first time they met, only a little flatter. She was going as Wednesday Adams.

Pinn assured her he would die before he let her leave the planet. Hermine thought that a little dramatic and that's what they were discussing as they wandered back to the compound where they were seen through a telescope by Sugar from the terrace of the west wing.

Sugar had gone to the terrace to stretch, breathe, exercise, and relax. There was a telescope there. She began her routine. She breathed in, did three left, mindful wrenches, upright with her hands on her hips. Then three right the same way. She breathed out to a count of twenty four and while she did she took six, slow steps backward or forward, she did it alternately, and raised her arms skyward. On the last step she brought her arms down and began breathing in again, consciously, to a count of twelve, wrenching left and wrenching right. She did that nine times and was happy with her workout but touched her toes breathing freely three times at the end just in case.

She was about to leave when she remembered the telescope. It was pointed upwards at clear blue sky. She lowered it to view the barrenness before her and was just about to quit when something flickered in her peripheral vision, left. Not through the telescope but out side of it. She focused the telescope on the position and was mortified to see Pinn and Hermine leaving the billabong. They were talking with some animation, and one touched the other.

*

Snake was alone when Pinn returned to New Cubus after leaving Hermine.

"Where are the others," he asked?

"Izabella needed help with holograph ports and autobot spiel for the party," said Snake, swiveling his chair Pinnward.

Pinn offered coffee. Snake accepted and Ramone appeared seconds later with a cup for both. She knew what was coming and quietly took a seat.

"We did not talk much about Hermine earlier,' Pinn began, mainly because I did not want to talk about her predicament in front of everybody else."

"Secrets already," said Snake, we are not off to a good start, are we?"

"Strategy"

"Semantics, you want me to do a little time whispering."

"Yes, I do. At the close of the event tonight, shortly before Shamash leaves, Izabella has scheduled two humorous and clever skits to be performed on separate small stages on the path out to close the festivities. They will not be more than four minutes long. Conveniently, she has decided she needs a third skit, something about balance she said, and I would be indebted if you would do it. Let the Indian rope trick be the third, the last act. I would like the disappearee to be Hermine of course, providing where she disappears to is not interplanetary."

"Anything else?"

"No, that should do it. You can have eight minutes if you need it."

"It took twelve the last time I did it," said Snake," she might only disappear from the thigh up."

Pinn took that as agreement and explained Hermine did not know of the plan yet. "The show," he said, "had to finish as close as possible to Shamash's scheduled departure. I'll fix that with Izabella."

*

After seething as long as she could stand seething, Sugar sent for Hermine.

Hermine was not happy and blurted out, "what," as she approached her mother who had returned to the southern terrace and taken a seat on a divan by a handsome pygmy date palm just about to fruit.

"Settle down sweetheart," responded Sugar, "take a seat, have an iced chai."

"I don't want an iced chai mother, or a seat. I want to return to what I was doing before I was dragged away. What do you want?"

Sugar pointed to the telescope a few meters away and told Hermine to go and look into it. She advised her not to move it, just look through it.

Hermine did as she was told. She looked through the telescope for a few moments and then returned to her mother. She took a seat opposite, poured an iced chai, settled back, crossed her legs, but said nothing.

Since Hermine was not forth coming, Sugar began to ask questions about what she saw through the telescope and established Hermine knew the spot. The path leading to and from the billabong.

Sugar waited for Hermine to go on but when she didn't, she did.

"A couple of hours ago I came out here to stretch and breathe so I would be suitably grounded for tonight's events. Anyway, after I had finished, I noticed the telescope and thought I might take a peek. I saw you and Pinn leaving the billabong talking with animation, and at one stage, you even cupped Pinn's elbow."

"He's my father, mother, there was a rock in his path, I was not sure he saw it."

"Ok, but you two seem to have a suspension of disbelief thing happening when it comes to knowing what one is to the other."

Hermine uncrossed her legs, leaned forward and placed her elbows on her knees. Her hands were clasped in front.

"Let's not talk about your problems mother," she said, "let's talk about mine. I don't want to leave."

There was a long silence during which both girls felt the ground shake, then Sugar said, quite casually, "Nor do I."

"Nor do you, what," asked Shamash as he entered the terrace?

"Consider cinnamon the aphrodisiac it is purported to be," replied Sugar.

She rose and offered the divan she had been sitting on to Shamash. She took a seat nearby. Shamash remained standing.

"We were just discussing the recipe they use for chai in this part of the universe."

Shamash grunted, then, addressing Sugar said, "Gq endep Idules art defdee end xofint ate," which meant he would be occupied in otherworldly matters for the time being but would make himself available for an hour or so before departure so he could make an appearance at Pinn's Halloween party and meet the boy.

"The Earthlings will be disappointed," said Sugar.

"I doubt it," said Shamash. "If Sumonus is not present, I will have the place razed upon our departure."

*

Pinn had just come out of a meeting with Frank and Jacob when he ran into Catherine and John John exiting the elevator on level three.

The usual greetings were exchanged then Pinn tried to excuse himself. He said he was late. He was meant to catch up with Bruce in about five minutes by the pool.

"This will only take a minute," said Catherine. "I am your wife."

"You should mention that to John John," said Pinn.

Catherine snarled but did not bite. She too was in the middle of styling herself for the party. She was going as Cruella. John John loitered a short distance behind. He was going as Indiana Jones.

"We are a little over seven hours away from lockdown," Catherine said steadily, "and there is still no decision about whether John John can stay or has to take the midnight rocket to Sydney."

"He can stay," said Pinn.

Catherine threw her arms out, embraced her husband, and gave him a big kiss.

"Did you hear that darling," she said turning to face John John? "You can stay."

Turning back to Pinn she asked, "When did that happen?"

Pinn described the morning they went out riding and how John John unwittingly discovered something he shouldn't have and when given the choice of whether to stay and say goodbye to everything he had ever known and abide by a few strict protocols, or have his memory wiped and go on as if nothing ever happened, he chose to stay. Not being the trusting type, I also imposed the memory wipe. The latter action did not negate the former agreement, so, since the end of his first visit John John has been an official Petalgeuseian."

"You could have said."

"You were busy, and he's proved useful otherwise."

"In that case," said Catherine, "there is something else we need to discuss with you. It's urgent."

Pinn reiterated he was late and instructed her to speak to Frank. "Frank coordinates. Tell him what it is you want or what you need. He will tell me, and we will decide once Shamash has departed."

Pinn bid them farewell before any objections could be raised and hastened down the hall to a western transfer station.

*

Pinn need not have worried about being late. When he arrived poolside, Sugar and Hermine were sitting at Bruce's table and whatever joke they were sharing was obviously hilarious.

Pinn apologized nonetheless for his tardiness and asked what was so funny as he took a seat.

Bruce said he was telling them the story of Raggot's Armageddon.

Pinn said he didn't know that one.

The girls stood almost immediately after Pinn sat, still chuckling a little. It was after five and they had to go and finish preparing for the party. They said they would see him later. Sugar cupped Pinn's face, kissed him on the cheek and looked into his eyes with concern. Hermine kissed him on the lips and skipped off to join her mother.

"Are you ready for this," asked Bruce?

"I am hoping so," said Pinn, "but right here, right now, I am feeling emotional."

"Well, snap out of it," said Bruce, "this is no time to get maudlin. You have a big night ahead and survival is at stake. Get emotional after you succeed."

"I have never been tested," said Pinn. "I have all these ideas about who and what I am in my mind that may or may not be true. I fear judgment is approaching."

"It's not approaching," said Bruce, "it's here."

He got up and went to the bar. He came back with a sweet white tea which he placed in front of Pinn.

Bruce told Pinn that due to a demarcation issue in the Wolf Star precinct of Idules, Shamash would not be attending the party as scheduled but will make a short appearance just before we are due to launch. That's both a good thing and a bad thing."

"Why?"

"Will Sumonus be available to meet Shamash?"

"I said he would be present at the party."

"Bruce told Pinn Shamash told Sugar he would raze Petalgeuse after his departure if he did not meet the boy."

"He could anyway," said Pinn.

"Sugar also said she wanted to stay on the planet along with her daughter and that she would break the news to Shamash when he returned to make his farewell.

Pinn suddenly felt like he lost consciousness, his whole life flashed before his eyes.

When he recovered, he said, "you got us into this Bruce. You get us out."

"I can't," said Bruce. "You have to do it. As you told the big guy last night at the BBQ, you are the captain of this ship.

"This is goodbye from me," said Bruce. "You are on your own now."

"Am I going to die?"

Bruce did not acknowledge the question. "I am leaving," he said instead. "From here I am going to the launch site, and you will not see me again. I wish you well Earthling. I would like to say you were my finest specimen, but you were not. He is yet to survive, and it is incumbent on you to see that he does. For that reason, I need you to consider a couple of things tonight.

"You were once Sugar's lover. Gods are generally jealous of their consorts' ex-lovers regardless of time. In my opinion, Shamash has shown admirable restraint regarding the matter so far. But now Sugar has chosen to stay with you and not accompany him and his rocket into the twilight, I doubt that will continue. With Hermine jumping ship also it could feel like a mutiny to Shamash and he may seek retribution. I can't see him killing the girls which leaves him only two other choices. Yourself or Sumonus. He may opt to kill you both, but my bet is he will go for the boy. He will be obvious. Men of power don't need imagination."

17.

The evening tiptoed in. Just as dusk dwindled, a single fireworks rocket burst with a boom, into a giant witch on a broomstick high above Petalgeuse. It held its shape to oohs and aahs before twinkling away.

Izabella got up on the stage, welcomed everybody to the event, said she was dying to officially start the party but first, the old man wanted to say a few words.

Pinn thanked everybody for coming, evoked a round of applause for Izabella and her team for the magnificent setup, and commented on the effort some had put into their costumes. "Have a spooky time," he said before decreeing the next day, November one, a public holiday.

There were cheers, Izabella nodded, and the band started up low and slow with an ominous beat.

The party began half an hour late and the boys, the Batman and the Hulk, who had already been at the party for half an hour considered 7 pm to be the start of their two-hour window.

After a while, as people nibbled and drank, the noise level rose to total engagement. It was carried sometimes by the band, or a squeal of surprise, but otherwise the observation held true.

They danced, they played games, a good time was being had by all.

At 7:45 pm Shamash's shuttle could be seen returning from the launch pad.

*

Unexpectedly, Shamash was not at all phased by either girls' decision to stay when the news was broken to him. He threw himself onto his designer day bed and guzzled a flagon of wine.

Getting to his feet a few minutes later, he called for his royal robes. "It is time to say goodbye to the Earthlings," he said.

Fitting the royal robes to a man nine feet tall took three valets and several ingenious lifting devices twenty minutes to accomplish. The gold epaulets and armbands, the heavy hat, the elaborate tunic, the high strapped sandals, the exquisite bulletproof apron with its ceremonial golden dagger hanging from its waistband were only the obvious intricacies of the ceremonial attire. He looked every bit a king as he strode across the southern courtyard.

For a while, they all thought Shamash was not coming to the party because almost immediately after the shuttle arrived back at the west wing two of Shamash's attendants accompanied by what looked like a puppy pallet jack collected the throne and took it to the shuttle. A few minutes later the shuttle set out for the rocket site. However, it returned almost immediately.

Everybody felt Shamash coming. The ground shook. Pinn stepped forward to greet him. Folks stopped what they were doing.

"Happy Halloween," Pinn said to the giant. "Welcome to our humble party."

"It doesn't look like much of a party to me," said Shamash. "Except for the bunting."

Pinn looked around at the suddenly still and quiet venue and agreed with Shamash.

"Where is the boy," Shamash asked Pinn?

From a distance behind and to Pinn's left, his son said, "here."

The Batman, Sumonus, was standing next to his mother, Michelle. His sister, Justine, who was playing his Robin was on his left, and Sugar was beside her.

It was surprising how similar Sugar and Michelle looked physically. They framed the scene. Blonde, shapely. A detail that did not go unnoticed by Shamash. Despite it being

Halloween, they were the only two wearing white. They both chose neck to heal robery in a light fabric that worked with the breeze. One's waist piece was silver, the others was gold.

Shamash laughed derisively, "A mummy's boy. I should have beheaded the portender of such a ludicrous prediction."

He was handed a flagon of wine by an attendant which he glugged down in one go. It got applause from a few in the bleachers.

"Come here boy," said Shamash. "Let's have a look at you."

Pinn turned to give Sumonus permission to approach but the Batman was already on his way, cape flaring. Robin followed but Sugar chased after her and took her back.

The Batman stopped about four feet to his father's left and stood legs apart arms akimbo.

"Take off your mask boy," said Shamash, "show me your face."

Pinn interjected and told Shamash avatars could not reveal their faces before midnight on Halloween lest their demons permanently inhabit them. As an example, he was going to tell the story of D. B. and the Esqua but glancing left he noticed the Batman had already done it. Removed his mask.

They stood six meters from Shamash. As Shamash's sharp green gaze met Sumonus's cool, clear, young one, Pinn felt an unhealthy bond growing.

He walked over to his son and stood between him and Shamash breaking the glare fest. He quietly instructed his son to put his mask back on, bow, and tell Mr. Shamash it had been a pleasure to meet him, excuse himself, and return to the bat cave. Don't stop, don't look back."

"Yes father. He called me a sissy."

"No, he called you a mummy's boy. His problem."

Pinn went back to his place.

The Batman did as he was told and left. Robin went with him.

Shamash was not quick to temper but he did feel he had been slighted by the boy's abrupt departure. Like father, like son, he thought.

Pinn apologized for his son's actions, blaming himself. He said the boy was OAC, out after curfew, and wished to avoid further punishment.

Shamash paced. He called for another flagon of wine, drank it and paced some more. It was a good thing he had a crew to fly his rocket out that night Pinn thought. Questionably, suddenly, Shamash calmed.

"Perhaps I have been an ungrateful guest," he said. "I need to return to the west wing briefly to say goodbye to the girls, but I will be back. Have your family, including the children gather at the shuttle staging in fifteen minutes. I would like to thank you all personally for your generous hospitality."

18.

Here is where our story ends, not the whole story, but the part we are telling.

Shamash took longer than he thought he would at the west wing. Sugar and he got into a tempestuous argument.

215

Thunderbolts and lightning. Very, very frightening. It was heard by all. So he was running late when he returned to the shuttle. He greeted no one. It was obvious he was perturbed and in a hurry. People moved back.

Just as Shamash was about to step onto the craft, he stopped and gathered himself. He took two steps backward and turned to his right. The Batman stood before him. Without hesitation he stepped forward, withdrew his ceremonial dagger and stabbed the boy between the third and fourth rib on his left side with such force that the lad was launched onto a low hedge a few meters away.

Shamash passed the bloodied weapon to an attendant as he boarded the shuttle.

Minutes later Shamash's rocket ceased to exist. There was no blast off, it simply vanished.

*

During their initial discussions when they formed a human dome, Pinn presented a vague plan to give them options if Shamash decided to try and harm Sumonus. Key to his strategy was that both Sumonus and he have doubles.

Frank volunteered Jacob for the role of Sumonus, the Batman. He said he had body armor he could wear under the costume that nothing could penetrate. He suggested when Sumonus readied his costume for printing he should add a little height and bulk.

Michelle said she'd take care of that.

Deciding who would play Pinn was much harder. After bandying a few names around they decided on John John.

John John was about the same height as Pinn with the same hair, only thicker, and features, only finer. Frank said Jacob would have body armor to fit him too.

Pinn had to agree with the consensus, but he was not happy with John John playing him.

"I don't think I will be a target," said Pinn, "but if something happens to me, John John should not be able to assume my position regardless of what Catherine says. Frank has been our captain now for three years; there should be no change."

When Pinn sent Catherine and John John to Frank, Frank asked John John if he would mind being Pinn's double for the evening. It didn't mean he could not enjoy the party, all it meant was he needed to be available to make a quick character change if required. John John was comfortable with the request and Frank's assurances he would be safe. Catherine was not. Frank explained it was unlikely John John would be called upon but in the scheme of things it was a necessary precaution.

Catherine mentioned her urgent matter again which, in the light of John John's cooperation, she expected to be addressed with appropriate alacrity after the event.

Frank said he would talk to Pinn.

*

Pinn thought Sumonus' meeting with Shamash went as well as could be expected. He was happy when it ended and Sumonus left. There was relief. But then Shamash issued the request that Pinn's family be present at the shuttle for his departure.

As soon as Jacob, already dressed as the Batman, received word he was required to impersonate Sumonus at Shamash's departure he set out to fetch Robin from the bat cave. She would need to accompany him upstairs. From New Cubus, Snake advised Sumonus Jacob was on his way and that Robin should be ready.

Sumonus was aware of the plan to present Shamash with a double if a second meeting was unavoidable but saw no reason for the deception. It was his opinion he should represent himself no matter what the occasion. With the flick of a switch, Sumonus set his door touchpad to incapacitate and a few minutes later Jacob lay unconscious on the floor just outside the bat cave.

Jacob's physical state registered in New Cubus and an alarm was raised. The bat cave, normally the boy's room, was isolated. No one in or out. Pinn was alerted.

They had seven minutes until Shamash was due back.

The best idea Pinn could come up with after arriving at the boys' rooms was that he play Batman. The suit was big enough and Justine could do the makeup. When he first got the suit on, he thought he would use Jacob's body armor, but after stuffing it in, he looked quite porky. He took it out. Shamash would notice a paunch.

Michelle, Catherine, and John John had been alerted also, so the bat cave was getting crowded. Catherine made John John look like Pinn. Jacob's body armor was perfectly disguisable in John John's makeover.

Sumonus protested, "I am not afraid father."

"We have already had that discussion," said Pinn in his stern father's voice.

Michelle, stood behind the boy with her hands on his shoulders. Returning her husband's gaze she said, "your father is right son."

*

There is no describing the shock, horror, confusion, and despair in the seconds, the minutes, and the hours after Shamash dispatched Pinn.

Shamash left the planet thinking he'd killed Sumonus and did not raze it.

Later in the evening, Michelle sat quietly at Pinn's favorite table by the pool. She looked out over the barrenness, which was just flat black by then, not counting stars. She was joined by Ramone.

"What I don't understand," said Michelle musefully, "is that Pinn's Zi was supposed to protect him. According to Bruce, Pinn's Zi came with twenty-five thousand years of life and various other benefits. What happened?"

Ramone said Pinn's Zi was a placebo, a trick, something manufactured to induce commitment. Bruce was worried Pinn was lacking self-belief and thought a test might resolve the issue. Zi. Firstly, Pinn had to insert it, which meant he had to deny a belief he had held all his life. Secondly, he had to be convinced it would fulfill all Bruce said it would. To that end, upon insertion, the device delivered a managed dose of a modified ephedrine. It gave Pinn the rush and the thrill needed to imply the sudden arrival of power. And it influenced you too, when you touched it. The drug wore off of course and was only delivered again, thereafter, in smaller doses, on the odd occasion. Bruce reckoned the ruse worked."

The End